Loyalty Over

Everything Else

Anjela Day

&

Raymond Francis

Loyalty Over Everything Else

Kre

Where I was from, life was not to be taken for granted. I was a youngbul, but I had already experienced some shit in my lifetime. Living in the West Park housing projects in West Philadelphia, every day it was something. Philly was crazy and bodies dropped on a daily basis like we were in Iraq or something.

I was 15 years young and lived in an apartment with my little sister Kenya, who was 14, and my mom. We were a pretty close family who didn't have much, but had plenty of love for each other. We all had hustler's mentalities so we had more than most families in our projects. I also had an older brother, Keon, but he didn't stay with us anymore. Keon was the fuckin' man though.

Every time I saw my brother, he had on some new shit. Whether it was a new MK watch, a pair of

Gucci shoes, or a Billionaire Boys Club sweatshirt; Keon was always fresh. With the way that he was getting money, there was no reason for him not to be. Even though he was only 22, Keon was pushing more weight than most of the oldheads in our hood. I didn't know exactly how his hustle worked, but I knew that he was getting paid and that was all that mattered. Keon said I was too young to run with him and his squad, but the way I saw it, money didn't have an age. I was almost 16 and in my sophomore year at West Philadelphia High, and as far as I was concerned I figured that I should be hanging out with my brother and his homies by now.

Even though I was ready to hit the streets, my mom wasn't ready to let loose of me just yet. She had already given up on Keon though. It wasn't like she didn't love him, but my mom had lost control of Keon a long time ago. He had been wilin' out since he was 13. While other kids were writing raps or dribbling basketballs working on their crossovers, all Keon ever thought about was getting money. In junior high, Keon was selling dime bags of weed on a daily basis. By the time he was in high school, Keon was running through ounce after ounce of crack. He always joked that he was the only student with more money saved up than most of his teachers!

Once Keon decided he was finished with school and started hustling full time, his money started flowing in even faster. He was getting it hand over fist, so of course he copped a wheel. It was a '2012 BMW 750li; all white, with chrome 22's on it. I never understood how he kept that whip so clean; he must have washed it every morning. Even after rain or snow storms, there was never a spec of dirt on that car. It was one of the hottest whips in the hood.

Loyalty Over Everything Else

Even though Keon didn't live with us anymore, he would still drop by to check on us and drop some money off at least once a week. Most of my days were filled with playing Playstation, watching basketball on TV, or arguing with my little sister Kenya; but the days that Keon came by were exciting. He always had stories to tell me about what had happened in the club over the weekend. Keon made the club sound like it was the best place on Earth. I had been to the little kiddie clubs before, but they didn't even serve drinks and they closed around midnight.

The clubs Keon was going to were official. He told me how he used to be at the bar in V.I.P. rubbing shoulders with everybody from Meek Mill to Philadelphia Eagles niggas like Michael Vick and Desean Jackson. Since I was too young to go, I had to live through my brother's club stories but I knew that when I was able to go to the club, I was gonna be the shit. I was gonna be fresh as hell, poppin' bottles and grindin' on all the thick-ass jawns on the dance floor!

My mom was real smart, but physically she was weak. She had all types of health problems, so instead of having a job, she got a disability check from the government. That money took care of the bills, but it didn't leave room for much more. If it wasn't for Keon, we would have been fucked up. However, my mom refused to rely strictly on her son's drug money and government assistance.

Since she was resourceful, my mom got herself a little side hustle poppin'. Every weekday morning, she turned our project kitchen into a mini fast food joint. She cooked eggs, sausage, and bacon for breakfast sandwiches and sold them to all the working people in our building. On a good day she made between $40 -$50 profit. It wasn't hard to see where we got our hustlin' mentality from.

My sister Kenya was an average 14 year old girl, annoying at times but still a cool little sister. She was pretty and even in loose fitting clothes; her body was still starting to show. I tried my best to look out for her, because I knew the niggas around our hood only wanted one thing from her. As far as I was concerned, she didn't need to be fucking anybody yet. Shit, I was a year older than her and I was barely having sex yet. Kenya was into doing Suduko, watching reality TV shows and could care less about having a boyfriend. I was doing my best to keep it that way.

Me and Kenya's dad had left the family 13 years ago so I don't really remember him. Keon's dad had been killed back in the day so we never knew him at all. My mom never hated our father, she just acted like he didn't exist; so after a while, so did we. I didn't hardly know anybody who had both of their parents, so to me growing up with just my mom was normal. Mom held me and Kenya down, and made sure I walked her straight home from school every day so that we didn't get into any crazy shit.

Living in West Park, there was always some sort of drama, but most of the time I stayed away from it. Every once in a while shit would pop off and I would get into little scuffles, but since Keon had taught me how to fight I was nice with my hands. I was calm and laid back, the only time I really lost my temper was when niggas disrespected my little sister; I hated that shit. Even though Kenya was a year younger than me, her body made her look like she was my older sister. Luckily, Kenya was quiet and shy, so most of the time we didn't get into any problems, but it my hood drama was inevitable. Living in the 'jects, it was only a matter of time before drama was bound to pop off.

Kalihia

Another day and I was just trying to make the best of a bad situation. My life was not sweet at all, but I was still thankful for everyday that I was blessed with. I lived in the West Park housing projects with my mom and to say we were struggling would be a compliment. We were damn near destitute, but we tried to make the most of what we had. We had to pinch pennies and make money stretch as much as possible, but that was life. What always seemed to make things even harder than they should be was the fact that my Mom had some drug issues that she was constantly dealing with.

As long as I could remember, my Mom had been struggling with her addiction. Maybe it was the fact that my father had done her wrong or maybe life was just too hard for her to cope, but my Mom couldn't stop getting high. It was some embarrassing shit to see her strung out stumbling through the hallways of our projects, but I had to live with it. The drugs had a bad hold on my Mom and I had come to accept it.

At 18 years old, I was a senior in West Philadelphia high school and just ready to be done with the high school thing. I got really good grades, but to keep it 100, my school wasn't hard at all. Teachers spent so much time disciplining disruptive kids that all I had to do was behave and they would reward me with A's and B's for making their jobs easier. Although I had good grades, college was more like a fantasy for me because unless I got a full scholarship somewhere, I couldn't afford to go. I tried to remain positive though and hoped I could make something out of my life, unlike most of the women from my 'jects.

While they were latching themselves onto the latest D-Boy to have a run in the drug game, I was trying to make my own way out. I had a little part time job at Black & Nobel book and record store that kept a few bucks in my pocket for time being, but I knew that wasn't going to get me out of Philly. For my long term plan, I actually I did have a nigga I was counting on for some help, but he wasn't in the drug game.

My boyfriend's name was Marshon, and this nigga was my world! He was 6'5, brown skinned, with curly hair and a lean, toned body. Marshon was in great shape because he was a ballplayer. He wasn't just a ride the bench player either; the nigga was a straight superstar who scored 25 a game. Marshon was on the radar of a few of the top schools in the tri-state, but hadn't picked where he was going to go just yet.

Wherever he picked, I was hoping to be able to follow him and live in an apartment off campus with him. It was a dream we had been keeping for the whole time that we had been going out. I felt a little guilty by using my physical qualities to get what I wanted out of life, but hey, God didn't give me these juicy tits, caramel skin, and thick ass thighs for nothing!

I liked the fact that Marshon didn't sell drugs or rob niggas, even though his big brother was known for both. Marshon was his own unique person, and besides him, the only other person I really fucked with was my BFF Rhonda. She lived in our projects too, and I was currently on my way up to her place so that we could ride out in my little Mazda squatter, which my uncle had given me before going off to the Feds on some gun charges.

Loyalty Over Everything Else

Rhonda never amazed me; why is it that when you make plans with black people, they are never ready? Now my ass had to climb a million stairs just to meet my home girl.

"Why the hell it got to be so many damn steps?" I questioned, as I walked up yet another flight of stairs.

I marched up the next three flights of stairs to my girl Rhonda's house. Rhonda had been my girl since third grade. We met at the bodega, when she didn't have enough money for the stuff her mother had told her to pick up so I gave her a few dollars. It might not seem like a big deal, but a gesture like that meant a lot in our neighborhood. Since then we have been like Thelma and Louise. She was my ride or die; with Rhonda by my side I was never worried.

I tapped on her front door, holding my purse tightly as a few fiends walked up and down the hall ways.

"Hey, what took you so long?" Rhonda asked standing in her bra and panties.

Rhonda was truly a pretty girl. She had naturally curly hair, was built like Toccara the super model, and the fact that she was a red bone didn't hurt.

"Are you kidding me? You ain't even halfway dressed yet?" I asked walking into the house.

I looked Rhonda up and down, pissed that she hadn't even started to dress. I walked straight to the kitchen, grabbed a glass out of the cabinet and washed it out. I reached in the refrigerator and grabbed the picture and poured me some Kool-Aid. I didn't even realize how thirsty I was until I was looking at the bottom of an empty glass.

"Damn bitch, save some for the fishes!" Rhonda joked, walking in the kitchen finally dressed in a black skirt with four inch heels and a low cup thin strapped top.

I looked down at my jeans and T shirt and rolled my eyes.

"Why you so dressed up? Just where are we going?" I asked Rhonda, placing my glass in the sink and walking towards the front door.

"To the mall. I wish I would walk out the house looking busted; too many boss niggas out here." she said.

I got the last laugh knowing that we had to walk down a million stairs, since the elevator was broken. I loved Rhonda, but we were nothing alike. She was that typical girl that lived in the projects that dreamed of meeting a trap star, getting married and living in Manhattan with the best of everything and never having to work a day in her life. I never thought that was possible, but Rhonda was convinced it could happen if she got with the right nigga.

I could never see how we got along so well being that I was a straight-A student that had dreams of going to college and becoming a success on my own and Rhonda was like a project diva. After all, I had lived in the same projects my whole life and seen so many of the dope boys come up in the game, make cash and then get killed over something as petty as a couple hundred dollars. I had to make it because I refused to be like my mother, who once was a very beautiful intelligent woman. My mom swears up and down that all her problems started when she met my father.

My mom says that my Daddy was a smooth talker that promised her the world, until he found out about her being pregnant with me. The day I was born was the last she ever saw of him. According to her, my father straight vanished into thin air like a ghost. That's when the pressure became too much for her and the drug use started. I knew that my mother secretly blamed me for the outcome of her life. I knew she felt that somehow she would have made it out of the ghetto were it not for me. Instead, she ended up addicted to a crack pipe, and became a woman that thought so little of herself that she would sleep with any man who paid her in order to feed that addiction. That damn sure was not the life for me; it just couldn't be.

*****

Before we made our way to the mall, Rhonda had other ideas. First we stopped at Mickey Dees and hit up the dollar menu. Rhonda was convinced that eating McDonald's a few times a week was what kept her ass fat and curvy.

> "I'm tellin' you, they put extra hormones in they food!" Rhonda would always argue. She was crazy as hell, but I had to love her!

After Rhonda scarfed down her food, we headed out to South Philly. She had been dying to hit up the tattoo shop. Rhonda had insisted on getting some lips tatted right above her ass, and since she had just turned 18, she decided it was the best time.

"Ain't you getting one?" Rhonda asked, with her face already turned up as the tattoo needle pierced her soft skin.

"No. I'm good," I said, browing through the tattoo book at some of the trifling tattoos that people had gotten in the past.

"Bitch, you need to lighten up and have fun, you act like we thirty years old or some shit. This is what we should be doing now," Rhonda said, making ugly faces as the artist dug into her flesh.

"Whatever," I said, as I walked away.

I wasn't concerned with getting a tramp stamp. Instead, I pulled out my phone and called the only person that I was always constantly thinking of.

"Yo," answered Marshon.

"Where are you at, babe?" I asked, loving the sound of my man's voice.

"Chillin'. Just hanging out with the team." he told me, and I instantly asked him to meet us at the mall.

Marshon agreed, and I couldn't wait for Rhonda to be done with that tacky ass tattoo so we could hit the mall up. Even if I didn't have money, I loved to walk the mall and just fanaticize about buying all types of shoes and clothes. I knew deep down that one day, I'd be able to afford anything I wanted out of the mall.

*****

We had been at the King of Prussia mall less than ten minutes and Rhonda already had set her eyes on some one, but the only dude I was checking for was mine. As soon as I spotted Marshon, a smile covered my face. He was with three of his ballplayer friends. Marshon was wearing a new Polo button down with some cargo pants and Timberland boots, on his preppy shit. He looked so good as he walked into my space. I could feel his arms go around my waist and I giggled loving his embrace.

"Hey babe," I said feeling his hands slip around my waist. He kissed my neck and I smiled.

"Hey Marshon," Rhonda said.

"What yall bout to do?" Marshon asked, still kissing my neck.

"I just came to hang out." I replied.

"Hey Marshon," some skeezer said, walking past.

He smiled at her like I wasn't even there. Then Marshon nodded his head at her, and for some reason, she got the balls to walk over. I sucked my teeth as this bitch.

"I'm coming to your game on Friday, can't wait to see you!" she said.

I wanted to swing on her. She had a lot of nerve walking up on my man like I wasn't even there.

"Bitch, you and a hundred other hoes! You don't see he is occupied?" Rhonda said, stepping over to where Marshon and I were standing.

"You know she broke with them Old Navy jeans on." taunted Rhonda.

Marshon and his boys laughed.

"What you should be doing is hitting us off with some cash so we can get fresh like you." Rhonda told Marshon.

"Oh ya'll need some money?" asked Marshon.

"We good babe," I told Marshon, but Rhonda was not about to let him walk away without giving me some cash.

"Like shit we is!" countered Rhonda, as she stepped in Marshon's face.

He released my waist and went in his pocket. Marshon handed Rhonda three bills and I cut my eye at her.

"Damn Marshon, your arms getting big as hell! Guess you been in the gym hard as fuck." Rhonda said, handing me two of the bills and walking away.

"You coming over tonight?" Marshon asked with hope in his eye?"

"No I need to study, baby."

"Shit Kalihia, if you need to study that much, maybe you dumber than you thought." Marshon said with venom in his tone.

"What is that supposed to mean?" I asked him, feeling way beyond pissed off.

"Shit, just that it's a million hoes that want to give it to me, and I'm trying to be with you, so what the fuck you always playing for?" Marshon said with the most seriousness in the world.

I looked away to see Rhonda looking at us with her mouth wide open. To say I was embarrassed was an understatement. I didn't even bother saying anything; I just walked away from Marshon and gestured for Rhonda to follow.

Once Rhonda and I got back to my car I could tell that she was upset, but no more than me. I unlocked my door and she grabbed hold of my arm.

"Look I know you waiting for that fairy tale type of love, but you a project, bitch. That shit not about to happen for us. You lucky to get a trap star and cash out, but yo ass got a ball player that is going somewhere and you afraid to give up the ass when he want it. This not the movies how long you think he gone wait, before the next bitch will be doing what you won't do?" Rhonda said walking away as if she was mad at me, for not giving up my pussy on demand.

I couldn't lie; Rhonda's words were burning a hole in my head. However, I didn't want to get pregnant and be stuck with a baby while Marshon was away at college, with the next chick. I saw what my mom went through as a single parent. Then again, maybe I was over thinking things. My mom had fucked up eighteen years ago. Nowadays, besides condoms, we had plan B and abortions. I really did love Marshon, and didn't want to lose him, so maybe I needed to go harder to please my man. I thought about that as Rhonda and I got another bite to eat and then headed back home.

Chapter 2

Kre

"Shorty! Yo, Shorty!" hollered a man from behind us.

Kenya ignored the man and just kept walking, but apparently he couldn't take the hint. We were just trying to get home from school and get something to eat, but this nigga harassing my little sister was making something as simple as that complicated.

"Damn, what's up lil' ma? Don't you hear me callin' you? Can I talk to you for a second?" said the man, as he left the other two men he was with and walked up on us.

"No thanks, I'm good." said Kenya.

"I'm sayin' though, what's ya name gorgeous?" he said, as he grabbed her arm.

Kenya pulled her arm away from the man, but he still kept trying to get at her.

"Yo my sister said she don't wanna talk to you. Get the fuck out of her face." I said, with a little extra bass in my voice.

That should have been the end of the conversation, but the man just kept drawlin'.

"Who the fuck you think you are little nigga?" he said.

The man was about 6'2, had a husky beard and smelled like weed. He was at least 20 and had no business trying to holla at my 14 year old sister. She may have looked grown, but she wasn't.

"I'm Kre." I finally answered, after sizing him up.

"Yo, that's Keon's little brother. Leave him alone, dog." hollered one of the man's friends.

"Nah man, fuck that. I should fuck this little nigga up since he got so much mouth." he said.

I don't know if he had a problem with my brother, or if he was just high, but this nigga just wouldn't leave me alone. I was scared and I knew shit was about to get ugly. We were only about 200 feet from the front door of our building, but it seemed like the projects were further away than ever.

"Go ahead in the house Kenya." I said.

"But..." she started.

"Just go ahead." I hollered.

I was hoping this would be one of those days when Keon's BMW would come pulling up, but my luck wasn't that good. As Kenya ran toward our building, I just kept grilling the man trying to show him that I wasn't scared of him even though I really was. At that point I knew my best bet was to try and catch the nigga off-guard, so I reacted on instinct. Keon had taught me that. All in one motion, I made a fist and then swung it at him. The first punch landed right on his jaw then I followed up with a left to his eye. It was a two-piece that Floyd Mayweather Jr. would have been proud of! The two punches stunned him and even stumbled him back a little, but they definitely didn't hurt him too much.

For a second both of us just stood there shocked, like we weren't sure what was supposed to happen next. I knew this nigga's pride was hurt; he wasn't about to be embarrassed in front of his boys. I also knew that I couldn't beat him, and even if I could, they were probably just gonna jump me. So after weighing all my options in a matter of seconds, I took off running like

Usain Bolt. Naturally, this nut-ass nigga started chasing me.

It seemed like it took forever, but eventually I made it to the front door of the building. Unfortunately, so did he.

"Come here lil nigga. Why you runnin?" he said, halfway out of breath.

I turned around and noticed that his homies had abandoned him, probably because they knew who my brother was and Keon had a reputation in the hood. As we both burst through the front door, I realized I didn't have time to wait on the elevator since he was only a few steps behind me. I figured I'd try my luck with the stairs. After all, he was a weed smoker so he would probably run out of breath way before I made it to my apartment on the 5th floor.

I ran up the stairs as fast as I could, pushing my way past neighbors who were on their way down, but I just couldn't shake this nigga. Part of me wanted to turn around and just fight him, but when I glanced back I noticed he had a knife in his hand! It wasn't just an ordinary knife either; it was a butterfly knife with a real long blade. I knew he wanted to shove that knife right into my gut or maybe even across my neck. Now, I felt like I was running for my life. This nigga was obviously crazy, so I couldn't lead him to my apartment. I definitely didn't want him knowing exactly where I lived; then he could come back the next day and get at me. I just kept running, even though I knew that eventually I would run out of stairs.

Before I knew it, I was on the 19th floor and there was nowhere else to go. I could hear his footsteps as he got closer and closer. Finally, I pushed the door open that led up to the roof. I was hoping there would be some shit up there that I could grab and use as a weapon, like a pipe or something. Unfortunately, there wasn't anything useful on the roof. As I stood on the rooftop and waited for this maniac, all types of thoughts were going through my head. I wished I was strapped and I could just pop a shot right between this nigga's eyes. I was quickly starting to understand why there were people like my brother and his friends who kept their guns on them at all times.

As I thought about the power of having a gun, I heard the door to the roof open.

"Ain't nowhere left for you to run now, youngbul." he said.

Then the man ran straight towards me, with the knife still in his hand. All I could see was that long ass blade, aimed straight at my stomach. Quickly, I made a juke move, like a running back dodging a tackler. I never played football, but I guess I would have been pretty good because the fake totally fooled him. He completely missed my upper body, but his foot tripped over mine. His momentum carried him past the spot where I had been standing.

"Shit!" he screamed, as he tried to regain his balance.

However, he was going too fast to stop. His body kept traveling forward and as I turned to look at him all I saw was the bottom of his shoes. He fell off the roof! We were 19 stories high, so I knew it was a wrap for him. In a matter of seconds his body would be splattered all over the parking lot and he would be dead. I didn't even bother to look over the edge of the building; I just got myself together and ran back inside. I was moving down the steps of the staircase at what seemed like the like the speed of light, not stopping for anybody or anything.

"Watch where you going!" I heard a girl's voice say as I bumped past her.

I didn't even look up to see who was hollering at me. My mind was racing and all I wanted to do was get back into my apartment. A man was dead and I wasn't trying to be connected to that incident at all. Everything was a blur, but before I knew it I was bursting through my front door. I put the chain lock on and ran straight to the bathroom. I felt like I had to throw up, but I couldn't, so I just stared at myself in the mirror.

After about 15 minutes, all types of sirens were blaring from ambulances and cop cars. It seemed like the whole projects were outside, looking at what remained of the man's lifeless body. I felt sick to my stomach, but I still couldn't throw up. The cops were asking the neighbors if they knew what happened, but since we all lived by hood rules nobody said shit to the police; not even the neighbors who had seen him chasing me up to the roof. After about an hour, they put up police tape around the scene and scraped his body off the pavement. I still couldn't speak; it was like I forgot how to move my lips or something. I just sat on the sofa and looked at TV, trying to fall asleep.

Kalihia

This youngbul Kre had just just bumped right past me without even stopping. That lil' nigga was cute, but he was weird as hell sometimes. I mean damn, here I am with these 36C cup titties halfway hangin' out of my shirt and these tights stretched over all this thickness and this nigga don't even stop to speak? What the fuck a bitch gotta do to get noticed?

I chalked Kre's rudeness up to immaturity and kept it moving up to Marshon's apartment. I was gonna surprise him and let him get a quick nut off before his game; he said that made him play better. Rhonda was right; it was time to stop rationing out pussy to my man. Marshon was a true testosterone filled, athletic Alpha-male type of nigga. He was always horny and tried to fuck as often as humanly possible. My sex drive wasn't as high, but I decided that I had to do what I had to do to keep that nigga happy.

Marshon was a catch, and truth be told, I was lucky to be fuckin' with him. I mean, like I said, Marshon was one of the top high school basketball players in the whole state. Every week they were writing about him in the papers and the whole city knew who he was; but I was the one lucky enough to claim him as my man.

Marshon was my ticket out of Philly. I had been stuck in the same projects that my mom was raised in with the same roaches, the same fiends, and same trifling ass people. Since I was ten years old I had the same goal; get the hell out the hood. Staying focused and going away to school was my original game plan, but my mother and Rhonda insisted shit didn't happen that easily and I was starting to think that they were right.

Maybe the only way out was getting with someone with a definite future. I thought that maybe I could be like my Rhonda, and meet a guy to spoil me. She fucked with a college nigga who eventually went overseas to play ball and now he sends her a little piece of his check every month. She hardly gets to see the nigga, but at least that money be coming in. So with a nigga like Marshon feeling me, how could I not play my part?

"Hey Miss Jones." I said, as Marshon's mom let me into their tight ass apartment.

Now, Mrs. Jones was a trip. She smoked so much weed that she didn't know if she was coming or going. Not surprisingly, she had a lit Dutch in her mouth as she let me in. She was smoking some loud too! I figured that she got that from her oldest son, who was a street nigga known to have good marijuana.

"Where Shon at?" I asked.

Miss Jones didn't even say anything; she just kind of motioned me toward the short hallway that led to his room. Miss Jones treated Marshon like a roommate more so than a son. She let him come and go as he pleased and have company at will. I had never dealt with a nigga whose Mom didn't care if he was in his room getting some ass while she sat right in the living room, but that's how Miss Jones was. I could even sleep over Marshon's apartment if I wanted to as long as I wasn't in the bathroom when his mom was trying to get in there. As long as she was high, didn't shit really bother Miss Jones.

I strutted my thick, sexy ass down the hallway and turned the knob on Marshon's bedroom door. However, I was thrown off as I heard someone else's voice coming from inside the room. Marshon was a freak, so I figured that he was probably watching a porno. I didn't want to just bust in and embarrass him, nonetheless I thought maybe if I peeked in and watched a little, maybe it would be easier for me to relax.

I cracked the door, but to my surprise, Marshon was laid up with some bitch! All of a sudden I was wondering why the hell I had even come there unannounced. How dumb could I be to think this nigga could be faithful? Seriously, Marshon was all-state in basketball, and was on his way out the hood. Bitches were throwing pussy at him left and right and ain't too many men gonna turn down some free ass.

Tears were already running down my face as I heard the bitch moan out "Damn, Daddy!" I was hurting so bad that I didn't know what to do. I took a deep breath and started to turn around, but I couldn't. As painful as it was, I continued to peek in the bedroom looking at them all caught up in their selves.

Maybe I should go in and get in the bed with them, and show him I'm all he needs, I thought to myself.

That would show Marshon how real I am.

"Oh shit, you wet as hell today." Marshon said, completely oblivious to the fact that I was watching his trifling ass.

"It's always wet for you." I heard the female whisper.

The voice of the woman piqued my interest. It sounded familiar but when they rolled over, and the bitch sat on top of him, my eyes got big as hell. If the curly hair wasn't enough, the red lips tattooed on her ass were a dead giveaway. I could see that the woman was Rhonda! Damn, she had been my home girl since I was nine. Words couldn't even form in my mouth. I wiped my tears with the back of my hand, ready to kill her. Rhonda must have thought because I didn't pop off like she did that I was a weak ass bitch.

My second thought was to push the door open and rip that bitch Rhonda off my man and toss her to the floor. I wanted to pound my fist into her face, like he was pounding his dick into her coochie. I could already feel myself chocking her up as she felt every bit of pain that I was feeling. She was my bitch since grade school! Rhonda had been smiling in my face, but the whole time, she was fucking my man behind my back.

"*Snake ass bitch.*" I thought, watching that fuckin tattoo bob up and down as she rode his dick.

I could feel tears well up in my eyes and I couldn't bear for them to run down my face anymore. Rhonda needed her ass beat. It wasn't like I wasn't fucking Marshon at all. I just wanted to wait until my finals were done at school so that I could make sure that I made it into a good school. Marshon should have understood that better than anyone since he was headed to college. The longer I watched, the madder I got. I was so close to taking my thoughts and acting on them, but lightly I closed the door back and made my exit.

Racing out of Marshon's bedroom doorway, I went past his high ass mother without saying anything. I needed to get the fuck out of that apartment. It was one thing for Marshon to be a dog, but Rhonda really surprised me. I couldn't even think straight as I speed walked all the way back home.

*****

After getting back in my apartment, I sat in my bed listening to my music as I normally did. Music had a way of crying for me, so I wouldn't have to. I know that may sound crazy, but since I didn't have Rhonda to talk to, or Marshon to chill with, music was my escape and I was using it. Yo Gotti's "Cold Blood" played in my ear and I pictured myself being free.

I just wanted to finally be out this hell hole. No more oodles and noodles, but instead shrimp and lobster. I could see myself buying the all of the things that I desired instead of five dollar leggings from the beauty mart. I wanted to be able to turn on the lights and not worry about the one roach that didn't run. A tear traced my face as I thought of being stuck in the hood my whole life.

As my bedroom door opened slowly, I looked at my mother, and sat up. She was looking a bit different than normal. I mean I was used to her looking a bit spacey, but this time she looked on edge. In fact it looked as if my mother had been crying. She closed the door and leaned against it.

"Hey, momma's baby." she said, walking towards me, talking to me like I was child.

Loyalty Over Everything Else

My mom sat beside me on my bed, and stroked my hair. I pulled away and grabbed my mother's hands. I loved my mother, but she hadn't been affectionate since I was five years old.

"You so pretty, Kalihia." my mom said.

I couldn't help but to raise an eyebrow as I thanked her. Something was up.

"How much do you owe?" I said, reaching into my nightstand to pull out the little money that I had.

"Like 40." she said.

I mean why else would my mother be in here, I thought while feeling defeated. Her eyes got even sadder as she took the money from my hand and tucked it in her bra. Then she kissed my forehead and stood to walk out the door. As she opened the door, she turned and looked at me.

"Kalihia, I will pay you back. You know that right?" she said, as a tear hit her cheek.

I nodded my head, watching her make her exit. My mom didn't have to say a word; her actions let me know what was up with her. She was back to using again, and there was nothing I could do about it. She was already in debt to her supplier. Me giving her the cash to pay for her fix was the safest way out of the situation. If she hit the street on her own trying to get some money, anything was liable to happen to her as crazy as our hood was.

The sound of my phone ringing broke my trance. I looked down and saw Marshon's number, wondering what he could possibly be calling for.

"What Shon?" I said trying not to sound mad.

"Come lay with me." he said, like he hadn't just cheated on me.

"Boy you can't be for real!" I wanted to say, but looking at my current situation I agreed to go up and see him.

I gathered my belongings and walked out of my bedroom. I walked past my mother, and she looked away. I looked at her, rolled my eyes and walked out of the door. I laid in Marshon's arms feeling dirty as he held me the way I loved. All I could think was that in this very bed, more than likely on these same sheets he was just fuckin Rhonda. Marshon had me in my feelings. My body felt cold on the inside, and even though I really felt better being in his arms, that was not where I wanted to be.

"What's wrong babe?" Marshon asked and I turned to him kissing his lips.

The first thing I thought was "Why you sex Rhonda? Am I not enough for you?" I wanted to ask, but

I knew he would lie and we would fight and I would just end up in tears. I knew if I confronted him that he would run to Rhonda and I would end up alone. Marshon was all I had and I didn't want to risk Rhonda being the bitch he wifed up, so I didn't say anything. I just turned to the floor, grabbing my purse and pulling out a condom, handing it to Marshon. He smiled flashing his perfect white teeth that I loved so much. He leaned in to kiss me again and I turned my head. Feeling the pain of penetration once again, he slid inside of me and I bit down on my bottom lip.

"You like that baby?" he asked.

I shook my head yes, while reaching down to run my finger over my clit. I really wasn't feeling sex; however I wanted this to be the best Marshon had ever had. He would be thinking of me every time another bitch was in front of him. I licked my lips rubbing my pussy; Marshon was going deeper and I had no choice but to take it.

I closed my eyes trying to go of all the hurt that I had felt. Marshon had fucked that slut, but he was mine and I was going to show him that my pussy was the best. I decided to sit up on my knees, slipping his pipe into my mouth, as I ran my fingers over my clit. His head fell backwards and his hands rose to caress my nipples. He pinched them both softly, causing my pussy to really get wet. I let out a soft moan and slid his entire pipe down my throat.

"Ahh," I moaned tasting the pre cum as he was now pounding the inside of my throat at the same pace that I was fingering myself. I bit down on my bottom lip allowing the cum to run down my hand. Without a thought Marshon tossed me to the bed and slid his dick back in me. I didn't have time to react, just grunt, feeling it in my stomach.

"Yeah baby," he said, kissing my neck as he went deeper.

Then he whispered in my ear, that my pussy was his. I closed my eyes tighter and allowed him to have his way with me. As good as it felt, I still couldn't shake my anger. He had fucked my best friend and I couldn't forget about that!

Kre

At school, shit was ridiculous. Even though people in my projects didn't talk to the cops, they talked amongst each other. Word had gotten out that a few people had seen me going up to the roof right before everything went down. All day, kids who never even spoke to me were asking me a million questions. I didn't answer any of them though, I just minded my business. Even my sister was looking at me funny, but she didn't say much to me.

When we got in from the crazy day at school, Keon was already at the crib waiting for us. I didn't feel comfortable telling anybody what had happened; except for him. Keon was like a God to me, like someone who was larger than life. I felt like if I went to him with my problems, he could make them go away. I took him into my room, locked the door and told him just what had happened. I told him that I was sorry for what had gone down and that I wished it had never even happened.

"Look Kre, I'ma be real with you. You ain't got nothin' to be sorry about. You did what you had to do, you feel me?" said Keon.

"But that nigga is dead though," I said.

"It's his own fault. You had to protect Kenya and yourself. You held shit down," said Keon.

"I feel like I killed him though. I got this feeling in my stomach that won't go away and every time I close my eyes I see his face," I explained.

"That feeling will go away. Just trust me fam," said Keon.

I was starting to feel a little better now that my big brother was around.

"But look Kre, since a few people did see you going up to the roof with him, I think maybe you'd better lay low for a while," said Keon.

"What you mean?" I asked.

"Why don't you just come stay at my spot for now?" said Keon.

Keon had been through plenty of crazy shit in his 22 years on the planet, so he knew what was best to do in a situation like this. My mom wasn't crazy about the idea, but she couldn't stop Keon from doing what he thought was best for our family. I packed a few bags of clothes and we loaded them into the trunk of the BMW. I hopped in the passenger seat, and we rode out. Keon was listening to Jay-Z's new album "Magna Carta Holy Grail" and every word that Hov said came through crystal clear with the custom sound system Keon had in his car. I think it was at that moment that Jay-Z officially became my favorite rapper.

Keon's spot was way out in Northeast Philly, about 30 minutes away from West Park. The first thing I noticed when we pulled up in front of his apartment complex was that there was really, really green grass outside. I didn't know what to expect of Keon's place, but I knew that if he had grass outside, the inside must be real nice.

Keon helped me carry my bags inside and get settled. Luckily, even though it was just him and his girlfriend Monique that stayed there, the apartment was a 2 bedroom jawn. Of course, Keon said I could stay in the extra room. He had a blowup bed in there that he said was for guests, but now it was for me. It didn't look too comfortable, but then again I doubted I would be able to sleep anyway since all I could think about was the way that man had flown off of the rooftop.

Keon's girlfriend Monique was real nice; she made me feel at home right away. Monique was about 5'3 with brown skin, a cute face, and a real big butt. I could see why Keon liked her; she was sexy as shit. On top of being attractive, Monique could cook her ass off. She made rib-eye steaks and sautéed shrimp with brown rice for me and Keon, and just a salad for herself since she was on a diet.

For the first couple of days at Keon's it seemed like all I did was relax, eat Monique's cooking, and play Playstation on the 55" big screen TV. Keon didn't do much either. Every couple of hours he would get a phone call and then he'd go out and make a run. I figured out that was when he sold his drugs. Slowly but surely, I was putting things together and learning just how the game worked.

Chapter 3

Kalihia

Over the next few weeks Marshon wanted sex more and more, but I just wanted to feel loved again. I really didn't want to be with him anymore, but I didn't want to be alone either. I laid next to Marshon as he was planting kisses on my neck and I was just lying stiff. He wrapped his hands around my waist and I closed my eyes. He was ready for sex; shit that's all it seemed like me and Marshon were doing lately. However, it was getting old and I needed a change.

At that moment, I knew that I couldn't give myself to Marshon anymore. The whole Rhonda situation was just too much. I sat up in the bed; Marshon didn't even move as I eased away and got dressed, as far as I was concerned we were a done deal.

"Where you goin Kalihia?" he asked.

I sucked my teeth and wondered was he for real.

"Home."

"Man here you go again!" he said, and I exploded.

"Here I go again, what? Guess if I don't fuck you the next bitch will. Who the next bitch? Who the next bitch Shon, Rhonda's ass? Huh? Yeah I know, I know, I know." I sung out, mocking Rich Homie Quan.

"What you talking about?" he asked, playing his dumb role once again.

I just wanted to go back to that day and kick both their asses. I stood up, put my shoes on and placed my hands on my hips.

"Nigga I saw you and Rhonda, and the fact that you didn't love me enough not to fuck my..." I started to say before my anger completely consumed me.

I was so enraged that I punched his stomach. I kept hitting him despite the fact that every time I hit him it felt as if I was hitting a brick wall. Marshon had truly hurt me and no matter what I did, it would never be the same. I showed out for a few more minutes, then got my shit and bounced. It was back to doing me and being the single Kalihia.

"Did his dusty ass really have to fuck that girl?" I thought.

How come he couldn't just man up and come to me? I would have made sure that he was satisfied.

"Fuck you, Shon!" I cried out.

Did he forget that we had our futures planed out? I just wanted it to work. Damn. I wanted Shon to love me! This was not how shit was supposed to go. I felt like I couldn't win for losing.

Kre

Before I knew it, I had been at Keon's spot for six whole weeks. I hadn't bothered to try and go back to school because I didn't see the point of it anymore. I was starting to get used to Keon's place and I liked being over there. I was only supposed to stay for a little while, but now I couldn't even picture going back to West Park. I was living good and I felt like I belonged at Keon's. Every single day, it was like I was learning something new. Whether it was a new slang word I was picking up on, some advice I was getting from my brother, or a new mixtape that I was hearing, everyday it was something.

Keon's squad of hustlers were all thorough. From their haircuts to their sneaks, everything was always fresh; especially when they headed out to the club. All of Keon's niggas were getting drug money and they made it look so easy. Some of them were getting more money than others, but they all were eating. It was like they were an NBA squad and Keon was the point guard. He made sure his team was always doing good; always ahead in the game like they were supposed to be.

Keon's right hand man was Wes. He was a few years older than my brother and was a tall, muscular nigga from somewhere in North Philly. Wes looked kind of like Michael Jordan, only he had hair on his head. He drove a black Chevy Tahoe, tinted out with deep dish chrome 26's. I wasn't really into trucks like that, but Wes' shit was hot. Wes usually came by the apartment like two or three times a week mostly to talk about business with Keon. I could tell they were talking about business because damn near every word they used seemed like it was in code. It was a drug dealer code that I was too inexperienced to decipher. All I knew was that just like Keon, Wes was all about his paper.

Shit used to really get hectic in our apartment around the end of the month. See, on the first, the government checks came out. So all the smokers who were on disability or welfare were ready to spend their money A.S.A.P. Keon and Wes always wanted to make sure they had plenty of work around for the first of the month because the flow got real heavy. It was the only time when I didn't really have much fun in the apartment. Shit was so frantic that Monique didn't even have time to cook dinner like she usually did. Everybody was too busy to pay me any attention, so all I could do was mind my business and try to stay out of the way.

It was at that time I learned that Keon didn't just keep Monique around because she was sexy; she was also a valuable member of his team. Monique knew how to weigh and bag-up drugs, as well as cook-up cocaine and baking soda into crack. Besides all that, Monique was also what niggas in the hood called a 'get-it-girl'. Get-it-girls were women who would take trips out of town either to pick-up or deliver drugs and money. Hustlers used get-it-girls because they were less suspicious. Monique's face was so sweet and innocent that no cop would ever think she was riding with a trunk full of cocaine and dirty money.

Monique didn't have a car so Keon used to get her rentals or buy her Greyound bus tickets so that she could go to New York and other places for him and cop weight from his connects. Once she got back into town, they would break down the drugs, bag them up, and supply their customers. Monique got paid pretty nicely for her part in the operation. At first I couldn't understand why such a sweet girl like her was mixed up in such a crazy lifestyle, but soon I figured it out.

One reason Monique was in the game was because she was definitely good at what she did. The other reason was that Monique had a taste for the finer things in life, and working a 9-5 was way too slow for her. She was into designer clothes and exclusive jewelry. Monique was too high class to wear the knockoff shit like everybody else. Just as fast as Monique made her money, she spent it on bracelets, rings, clothes, bags and shoes. She had a real obsession, but at least she was spending up her own money and not begging my brother for his. I had to respect her for that.

When Monique would make her runs out of town, Keon became a different person. Normally, he was only on the phone for business purposes, but without Monique around he used his phone to call up other girls. For each night that Monique was away, Keon would have a different girl come over and spend the night with him. The girls that he would bring to the apartment weren't nearly as cute as Monique, but he would still take them into the bedroom and knock them off.

I couldn't understand why Keon was cheating on Monique; she was so nice. She was only out of town for three days at the most, and as soon as she came back she was ready to have sex with Keon. I didn't understand how he could be that horny that he couldn't wait for three days. Keon just told me that once I got older and had a girlfriend, I would understand. He also told me that if I said a word to Monique about it, he'd beat my ass and I knew him well enough to know that he meant it.

Once Monique was on her way back into town, it was business as usual. First, Keon would make sure all the evidence of his cheating was cleaned up and then he would call up Wes. Wes would come through and he and Keon would divide up the drugs that Monique had brought back into equal shares. I would watch them weight everything out and I picked up on the fact that 2.2 pounds was a ki. I had heard the word ki or kilo before, but I never knew it was an actual unit of measure.

Keon peeped my interest in what he was doing, so every now and then he would explain certain things to me.

“See this right here is the most important bag of them all.” said Keon.

"The dime bag?" I asked.

"Yep. You might think we make money flippin' ounces, but we see more profit off of a dime than anything. When people buy more, you have to give them a discount. When they buy less, you can overcharge them." said Keon.

"So why not sell all dimes?" I asked.

Keon's answer was simple; he just pointed at the clock that was up on the wall.

"Time. It's the only thing that never stops. No matter how much money we make, time never stops, so we have to flip this shit as quickly as possible. I'd love to sit in the hood and sell 1,000 dime bags a day, but there isn't enough time to do that, ya dig?" said Keon.

It was a complicated principle, but I was starting to understand.

As I learned more about the hustle, Keon delegated a few responsibilities to me. I learned how to shave crack, weigh it up on the scale and bag it up. I started off doing the small bags of grams and worked my way up to bagging up ounces. It gave Monique some time to rest her hands, so she appreciated it. Of course, my big brother started paying me for my work. There was no set pay rate; he would just give me cash here and there every couple of days. On a good day I got more and on a slow day I got less. For me, it was perfect. I hardly left the apartment anyway, so I figured I might as well make money while I was sitting around. It gave me something to do on Friday and Saturday nights while everybody else was out at the club. I got so good at weighing up the work that I could even eyeball it after a while!

As I learned more about the game, Playstation started to interest me less and less. Video games were like little kid shit; crack was real grown-man business. I took the money I made and tucked it into one of my socks and stashed it under my blow up mattress. As the months passed, that sock got fatter and fatter. I never counted all of my cash, I just liked the fact that I knew it was there. Best of all, I never had to spend any of it. With Monique using her EBT card to get food and Keon and his friends handing me down their old clothes and hats, I had everything that I needed. I really loved my new life; I was becoming a true hustler.

While a sock was big enough to store my money, Keon was getting so much gwap that he needed a safe to keep all of his cash in. One day he went to the pawn shop and copped an all-black, fireproof strongbox and put it into his room. He didn't tell anybody the combination; he just put his cash and jewelry in there and locked it up. I knew at that point that my brother was a major player in the game.

Every night from then on, I'd notice as he would put more money into his safe. I was completely infatuated with my brother's lifestyle. From the way he always looked out the peephole in the door before opening it, to the way he ignored blocked calls on the phone, I imitated his every move. One thing I couldn't imitate from Keon though was how he kept his gun on his hip everyday all day, since I didn't have any heat. I wanted a gun bad as shit, but for time being I just admired Keon's.

As Keon got more used to having me around, he actually started taking me places with him. I would never be with him when he was doing anything drug related, but I started going out shopping with him and little shit like that. I felt like I was a real part of his team, and I liked that. Whenever we would go out to King of Prussia or Cherry Hill Mall, Keon would always grab me a Polo shirt or a pair of Chucks.

Sometimes we would go to 69th Street and watch movies, or go to Black & Nobel and buy all the new mixtapes and DVDs. I felt like I was doing it real big, especially to only be 15. When I would see people that I used to go to school with, I would make sure that they noticed me but I would never speak to them. I wanted them to know that I was getting money, but I didn't want them in my business. In my eyes, those little niggas who were still wasting their time in school weren't even on my level and couldn't relate to my life. I was grown and they were just young bucks.

Kalihia

The day seemed to be dragging. Standing at the front desk of my part time job at Black & Nobel, watching these lame niggas come in and out of the store trying to holler at me had me feeling frustrated. Truth was I wanted to go home, lie down and keep it moving. Somehow it seemed as all my days were starting to feel the same and I truly could use a change.

I had bent down behind the counter when I heard two men talking. They were laughing and one of the men sounded so familiar. I stood to my feet and realized who the voice belonged to. However, I couldn't believe it was Kre. The youngbul looked like a million bucks. He was rocking a striped Polo shirt, light blue Rock & Republic jeans and a pair of Air Max 95's. However, the clothes were not what was so sexy about Kre. It was his almond colored skin, his full lips that were now turning black, his dark brown eyes, but most of all his confidence. Kre commanded the room.

I stood straight up fixing my clothes, hoping to catch Kre's eye. He was standing next to his brother, who was looking equally as good, but for some reason I wanted Kre. He stood at the counter looking dead in my eyes, but it was like he was looking through me. He handed me the money for his music, and I made sure to caress his hand as we made the transaction, however it didn't move him.

Honestly, I think the fact that I knew that I was looking good and Kre paid no mind to my body made me want him even more. Or maybe it was the fact that he didn't want me, and lately men had only been using me. Nonetheless, I watched him and his brother walk out the door and I was feeling like I had missed my chance.

Fuck that, Kre was the type of nigga that I could upgrade. I could see myself on his arms, being the bitch that every female envied. Mostly I pictured the look on Rhonda's face seeing me with a nigga that was about to blow in the hood. I knew Kre was just a youngbul now, but he had stepped up in such a short time, I could tell that he was destined to be a boss, and I was gone be the bitch by his side.

Kre

Just like we did every Friday afternoon, Keon and I had copped our new music for the weekend and were at the barbershop getting our haircuts. Keon would always tip the barber $40 extra, so we had priority over the other customers and we never had to wait too long. It was part of our routine, but I would quickly learn that when you lived like Keon it wasn't good to follow the same routine every week. The money Keon was making made a lot of haters jealous, and a broke, jealous nigga is liable to do anything.

After we left the barbershop, we headed straight back to the apartment. I begged Keon to let me drive the BMW home, since the shop was only a few blocks away, but he wasn't with it. He trusted me, but not that much. When we pulled up outside the apartment, everything looked normal, but I could feel in the air that something wasn't right. I guess Keon felt it too, because he didn't say shit as we walked up to our door. Keon looked at our window and noticed that the lights were off, which was weird since he knew that Monique was supposed to be home. Keon was real perceptive like that; he paid attention to detail all the time.

As Keon slowly opened the door, he kept his hand on his gun. Then he stepped inside and flipped the lights on. The apartment was trashed; shit was thrown all over the place. The big screen TV was pushed onto the floor, the sofa was flipped upside-down and the phone cord was ripped out the wall.

"Mo! Where you at?" asked Keon, but there was no response.

"Yo, wait right here Kre." said Keon, as he pulled his gun off of his waist.

I stood right there, stiff as a statue. I didn't know what the fuck was going on, but obviously we had been robbed. I just hoped that Monique was OK. This was a part of the game that I just wasn't ready for yet.

Keon went into the bedroom and found his girlfriend hog-tied to a chair. Her mouth was gagged, so she couldn't even scream. Monique's face was beaten and bloodied, but she was alive. I helped Keon untie Monique, as she began to explain what happened.

"I heard a knock on the door, but I couldn't see anybody through the peephole. I opened the door a little bit, and two guys with masks on pushed their way in. Then they kept askin' me where the money was. I told them I didn't know the combo to the safe, so they beat me and tied me the fuck up." said Monique, as she cried the whole time.

The men didn't really get much, other than a couple hundred dollars Monique had on her, some of her jewelry and a few ounces of cocaine that were under the sink. Keon helped his girlfriend wash her face off and put peroxide and band-aids on her bruises and cuts. I knew right then that even though Keon cheated on Monique, he did truly love her. I could see the hurt in his eyes as he helped Monique into the bed. He wasn't mad about the coke he had lost, he was mad that Monique was hurt and he wasn't there to help her.

Keon didn't know who robbed the apartment, but he learned a lesson. Whoever was responsible for it planned their move off of knowing that Keon would be in the barbershop at that time every week. It had to be somebody that we saw in the shop all the time and who knew that Keon was getting that money. They had probably followed us home before, peeped where we lived and decided to test us. Now, Keon knew to be even more careful with the way he made his moves. The streets were definitely watching us.

Chapter 4

Kre

After about a month, or so, Monique's injuries healed up and things were pretty much back to normal. Before long she was back on her get-it-girl shit making runs out to New York, Baltimore, and even Atlanta. Keon and Wes were still hustling and still getting money. I was still making my little paper, but more importantly I was learning the game. To me, the education that I was receiving was way more valuable than anything that I could learn in a school.

For the first time since I had left West Park almost two months before; I went back for a visit. I missed my mom and my sister, and I wanted to see how they were doing. Me and Keon picked a quiet Thursday afternoon when everything was slow and surprised my mom and Kenya.

Kenya was doing well; she had gotten even more beautiful than she was before. Her hair was long and permed and her eyebrows were plucked real skinny. Kenya was definitely growing up real fast, but she was still pretty quiet. My mom was happy to see us, but I could tell she was worried about me. I told her I was fine, and everything was cool. The projects hadn't changed much, other than a few new families who had moved in since I'd been gone.

We ate a little dinner, watched some TV, and talked for about an hour. Then Keon gave Mom a few hundred dollars and we bounced. Visiting time was fun, but it was time to get back to work. I had crack to cut, weigh and bag, and Keon had customers to supply. Time was money and we couldn't afford to waste any.

I really felt like I worked for a Fortune 500 company, that my big brother was the CEO of. The fact that the product that we were selling was illegal didn't matter to me. Keon and Wes were businessmen, Monique was the secretary, and I was a paid intern. The Tahoe and the BMW were like company cars, and Keon and Wes' stuntin' at the club was a business expense. In my eyes, I was an important part of the company. I was learning on the fly, doing it way bigger than most 15 year olds.

*****

Kalihia

It sucked that I would be spending Valentine's Day alone, so when Marshon hit me up telling me had something for me I jumped on the chance to possibly get back with him. I really didn't want to be with him but it beat sleeping alone and the other dudes that I had been kicking it with really did nothing for me. Truth of the mater, I didn't really want to be like my mother or the rest of these hood chicks fucking men for money. I wanted a real relationship.

I don't know why I kept trying to make it work with Marshon, because he always seemed to let me down. Nevertheless, I agreed to go up to his apartment. As I walked in, he was sitting in the living room talking to his brother and a few of his boys. When I stepped into the apartment, his friends looked at me, and they all started to scatter. Marshon had a dumb look on his face and I really was not happy to know what he was up to.

He kissed my face and pulled me in to him. I really didn't want his hands on me but it felt good to be touched. He led me down the hallway kissing my body as we got closer to his bedroom.

"What's up Shon?" I asked, watching him undress me with his eyes.

"I missed you." he said slamming the door shut and pulling me down onto the bed.

That nigga didn't miss me; he missed my pussy. It was what it was. I couldn't front though; I needed some dick so I let him do his thing.

"You got a condom?" I said with grit in my voice."

Marshon smiled holding one between his fingers.

"I hope that's not all you made me come up here for." I told him rolling my eyes.

Marshon smiled and went into his pocket, handing me a necklace. He looked very proud of the necklace so I smiled and allowed him to place it around my neck. After we had sex that night, I laid in his arms convincing myself that it could work with Marshon. Maybe, finally I could get what I wanted.

Just as I started to fall asleep, a light shined in my eyes now and had me woke.

“The hell?” I said looking at Rhonda stand over me as I opened my eyes.

She had her hands on her hips and was rolling her eyes.

“What?” I asked smiling, watching her eyes travel up and down my body.

Marshon sat up looking at the two of us. I reached for my clothes and slipped on my shirt. I looked back at Marshon who looked as if he had gotten caught with his hands in the cookie jar. I stood up slipped my jeans on and rolled my eyes at Rhonda.

"Don't feel so good when he cheating on you." I told her as I put my shoes on and Marshon grabbed my hand.

"Babe..." he said as Rhonda looked at him, but charged at me.

She knocked me to the ground, and started to hit me in my face. I tried to cover my face with my hands but she started digging her nails into me. I grabbed her hair and started to dig, getting her to finally release me. She was so mad that saliva was running from her mouth.

Finally I got the upper hand, flipping on top of Rhonda. She was fighting hard, kicking and punching, so I lifted her head and banged it into the floor. Unfortunately, that didn't slow her down, so my next move was to grab the first thing I could feel for. I grabbed a school book sitting beside Marshon's bed and bashed it into Rhonda's head. I pulled myself up from the floor. I didn't even notice that Marshon was pulling me as I pulled away and screamed.

"Both of ya'll stay the fuck away from me! I mean it!" I said, gathering my belongings and making my way out of that place.

Kre

It was Valentine's Day and Keon and Monique were supposed to be going out, but Keon wasn't home yet and he wasn't answering his phone. Monique was pissed, and I guess she had a right to be. She was a good girlfriend, and she never asked for anything. All she wanted to do was go out to eat in a nice restaurant and drink some Moscato to celebrate the holiday and she couldn't even get that. I knew that my brother cheated on Monique, but I also knew that he wasn't grimy enough to be out doin' dirt on Valentine's Day. I kind of figured that something might be wrong, but I didn't want to say anything. In Keon's dangerous line of work, anything was liable to have happened.

Finally, after Monique had given up on her dinner date, the house phone rang. It was a collect call from Bucks County Jail. Keon was out making a sale and had gotten pulled over with a nice amount of cocaine on him as well as $1,200 in cash. It was nothing that a good lawyer couldn't get him out of, though. He was going to have to sit in jail overnight, but needed to be bailed out the next day after he saw the judge.

Early the next morning, Monique made a few calls and found out that it would take $3,500 to bail out her man. $3,500 wasn't shit the way my brother was getting money, I know for a fact he had way more than that stashed. The only problem was that nobody knew the combination to his safe! It wasn't like we could just call the jail and ask to speak to Keon either. Writing a letter to ask for the combination to the safe was too time consuming.

Instead, Monique called up Wes to see if he could loan her the cash, but he said he only had $900 to spare. That was the first time I ever looked at Wes differently. I knew he was getting money just like Keon, so I knew he had more than $900 to put up for bail.

Wes made up some bullshit excuse about having to pay his momma's mortgage, but I knew he was just being stingy. To go along with Wes' $900, Monique had $1,000 of her own money to put towards bail. I couldn't understand how Monique made runs out of town every month but she only had $1,000 to her name. Obviously, she really had a problem when it came to shopping, but that was her business.

Monique was upset over the whole situation, but she was already taking action to try and get some cash. That's what I liked about her; instead of sitting around complaining, she was trying to solve the problem. Monique was on the phone with her girlfriends trying to raise some money by offering to sell off some of her exclusive pocket books and shoes. The girls she hung around were all broke though, so her plan wasn't working at all. It was a sad sight to watch, but I liked the way she was willing to give up all of her material shit to get my brother out of jail. After watching Monique make a few more moves, I finally decided to speak up.

"How much more money do we need to get my brother out?" I asked.

"$1,600. I'm bout to call some of his other friends." said Monique, pitifully.

"Nah, it's cool. I got it." I said.

I didn't know exactly how much I had stashed in my sock, but I knew it was more than $1,600. I went under my air mattress and pulled out the sock. For the first time ever, I counted up my savings. I had $1,825; more than Monique, and all I did was bag up crack! I wasn't nervous about putting my money up; I knew my brother would pay me back as soon as he got out of jail. One thing Keon hated was owing people money. As a matter of fact he would probably pay me back and then toss me a few bucks extra, knowing him.

I handed Monique the $1,600 and she looked at me like she was surprised. She didn't even bother to ask me where I had gotten it from though. Instead Monique just got a ride from Wes up to the jail and posted bail. Just like that, the problem was solved. I had come through in the clutch.

After Keon found out that I had put up money for his bail, he paid me back right away. He paid all of us back, with %10 interest just because that was how he got down. More importantly though; Keon stopped looking at me like a youngbul. I went from being his little brother, to just his brother. Keon saw me in a whole different light, he knew I was someone that he could count on when shit hit the fan. From then on, our relationship changed. I was no longer a liability; I was an asset.

Keon also realized that he had to tell Monique the combination to his safe, in case of an emergency. The niggas that robbed the place could have killed her, if they had gotten mad enough about not being able to get my brother's money. Also, if Monique had known the combo to the safe, bailing Keon out would have been easier. It just made sense for Keon to give Monique the combination.

*****

Now that I was grown in Keon's eyes, he had me doing more shit to help out the team. More responsibility meant more money, so I was with it. Keon was never going to allow me to be out on the corner slangin' drugs hand to hand, but now he was sending me on missions that involved me actually being around drugs outside of our apartment. Since he was hot after getting arrested, Keon laid low for a while and had me and Monique out making local runs throughout the city. I was there to protect Monique so that nobody would try to rob her; kind of like her bodyguard.

I was only about 5'7, 160 pounds but the gun that Keon gave me made feel like a giant. It was a black .45 Ruger and it was beautiful. It was nearly new and had only been shot a few times. Keon showed me how to load it and bust it and I was hype. I loved that gun, I felt like I could take over the world with it. I cleaned it every night and slept with it under my pillow. Just like Keon, I kept it tucked on my waist all day long.

When Monique and I rode out, we were very careful and alert. She was a real good driver who knew the city like the back of her hand. Monique even got Keon to take the rims off of his car so that we would attract less attention. I thought that was a smart move, even though the BMW looked funny without the 22's on there.

Things always went smooth for Monique and me. The city of Philly was so busy, we just blended right in with the crowd and handled our business. We rode around and dropped off a quarter ki here, a half-a-jawn there, collected the cash and kept it moving. Drugs were moving out and money was coming in. I had money in my pocket and a gun on my waist; it was the best feeling in the world.

Being out all day selling drugs for Keon worked up a major appetite for Monique and I. After we would finish making our deliveries, Monique would go to the market and get some stuff for dinner. I hated walking around the grocery store with her, but Keon told me it was part of my job. He was real over protective of Monique since the robbery incident a few months back.

"You want baked chicken tonight, Kre?" asked Monique, as she looked at the food.

Before I could even answer, a hood ass woman walked up behind Monique and interrupted us.

"What's up Mo? How you been?" said the woman.

Monique turned around and looked at the woman, who was a hot mess. She was pushing a shopping cart with her two kids inside and was wearing an old ass Roc-a-Wear valore set. She had her head wrapped up, with curlers under the scarf.

"What's up Kintasia?" said Monique.

"Not much, just in here shoppin'?" said Kintasia.

"You still livin' down Da Bottom?" asked Monique.

"Nope, we live in Korman Suites now." said Kintasia.

"Oh. Are you still with your baby father?" asked Monique.

"No, I got back with Bone. Ever since he came home last year he's been playin' his part so I gave him another chance." said Kintasia.

"That's what's up. You still workin' in Home Depot?" asked Monique.

"Yeah, you know it. I've been there for four years now." said Kintasia.

"Nothin' wrong with that. Anyway, take care of yourself. I got to hurry and finish shoppin' so I can go cook. Bye." said Monique, as we walked off.

To me, it seemed like just a boring ass conversation between two women who knew each other, but it was deeper than that. I didn't notice, but Kintasia had a husky bracelet on her wrist and a nice ring on her finger. It was the same jewelry that Monique had gotten robbed for. Every question she asked

Kintasia had a purpose. Monique was like an experienced attorney, setting up a criminal who was on trial.

First she found out Kintasia lived in Korman Suites, right on the edge of Southwest Philly. Then Monique found out Kintasia was fuckin' with Bone, who was a known stick-up kid. Monique knew that with the $10.50 an hour that Kintasia made working at Home Depot there was no way she could afford that type of jewelry. She hopped right on the phone with my brother and told him that she knew Bone was one of the men who broke into the house and robbed her!

*****

That night, when we got home, Keon told Monique not even to bother cooking. Now that he knew Bone was responsible for the robbery, we had business to handle. For the first time ever, Keon gave me the keys to the BMW. I was nervous, but I managed to drive to Korman Suites perfectly. Keon just sat in the passenger seat silently. It was the only time we rode in the BMW without any music playing. Neither one of us said anything; we just concentrated for the whole ride.

When we pulled up outside the apartments, I wondered how Keon planned on finding this nigga Bone. The complex was big and we didn't even know which building they lived in. However, Keon did know that the cheaper suites were up front, while the more expensive ones were in the back. Knowing Bone's broke ass, Keon told me to park up front. I cut off the headlights, and we waited. No radio, no CDs, no talking; we just looked out the window and waited. Even as the sun started going down we just waited patiently. I was hungry and starting to get a little tired, but I knew better than to complain.

Finally, after four and a half hours, Keon leaned over a flicked on the headlights. All the way across the parking lot, a short, dingy, man was taking out his trash. Keon squinted to make out the man then flipped on the high beams to get a closer look. It was him!

"Keep the car running, Kre." said Keon.

Then my brother hopped out the whip, with his gun in his hand. Sensing danger, Bone dropped his trash bags and started running back toward his front door. Keon raised his gun and started dumpin' as he got up closer to his target. Shot after shot was blazing in Bone's direction! The flash from the gun seemed like it lit up the whole night sky. Bone dropped to the ground, and the shooting finally stopped. Keon paused for a second, then turned around and walked back towards me. Not ran, but walked. It was almost as if Keon wanted people around there to see him and know what he had just done. He wanted them to know what he was capable of if you fucked with him.

Keon got back into the car, tucked his hot gun back onto his waist and I drove us home. I must have run through three or four stop signs on the way home I was so scared. I had seen people get shot before, but that was the first time I'd ever seen someone get shot and killed. I started getting that feeling in my stomach again, like the one I had after the rooftop incident. This time though, the feeling didn't last as long. And when I closed my eyes that night, I went to sleep with no problem. I guess I was getting used to this shit.

*****

Keon laid low for two whole weeks after killing Bone. He stayed in the apartment and kept the BMW parked up just in case anyone had seen us coming out of Korman Suites that night. No matter what though, his hustle didn't stop. He rented Monique a Toyota Camry and we still rode around the city taking care of business as usual. I was with Monique for hours at a time; I even spent more time with her than I did with Keon.

Wes started coming around the apartment almost every day, sometimes just to chill and hang out. Usually Wes and Keon's conversations were all about business, but now his visits were just on some regular shit. He would come through and eat dinner with us, watch movies, and smoke a little weed with my brother. I figured he had broken up with his girlfriend because Wes had way too much free time on his hands.

After going to see a few attorneys, Keon spanked his little case from a few months back. The arresting officer hadn't read Keon his Miranda rights correctly so the case was thrown out, but it cost Keon five stacks in lawyer fees. Wes suggested they should party down at one the clubs on Delaware Avenue or Spring Garden to celebrate, so him, Keon and Monique started planning everything out. When my brother and Wes partied, they did it real big. They brought all the major D-Boys in the city out and all the hoes who were chasing them came out too.

They decided to go out on the same weekend as my birthday, so I knew this was my chance to finally ask my brother if I could go to the club with them. At first Keon started talking that shit about me being too young, but then he thought about the way I had been taking care of business for the past few months. Keon figured that if I could manage to move his drugs for him all throughout the week, I could handle a Saturday night at the club.

Technically, you had to be 18 to get admitted into the club, but when you had money like my big brother it was easy to make things happen. When Keon and Wes went out they tipped bouncers and bartenders, so people remembered their faces. People treated them like superstars, and superstars don't have to play by the rules.

Monique brought herself a new 24 karat white-gold bracelet with a little bit of ice in it and a form fitting Prada dress with a matching clutch bag so that she could look good for the celebration. Me, Keon and Wes brought Armani button-ups and hard bottom Gucci shoes, real grown man shit. I felt like this was going to be the night I had been waiting my whole life for!

Chapter 5

Kalihia

My frustration had been mounting over the past few weeks. I wasn't talking to Marshon or Rhonda even though they had both been calling my phone on some apologetic shit. I didn't want to hear what either one of them had to say. Even worse, my hormones were raging. I had gotten used to sex on a regular basis, and without it I was backed up. I decided what would be best for me would be to get out and shake my big ol' ass on a dance floor in a club somewhere. The way I was built, I was bound to find me a nigga rapidly.

Standing five feet, seven inches with thick thighs and ass for days, why anyone would cheat on me was crazy to me. I mean I was the type of girl any nigga would dream of. Maybe I was fucking with the wrong type of dudes. I needed a nigga that could not only hit that spot, but be proud that I was on his arm. I knew niggas cheated, but the fact it was with my best friend was crazy.

How foul of a nigga was he to fuck me like nothing was going on; that felt like a hit below the belt. In fact, it had me in tears many of nights. How funny was it now that both Rhonda and Marshon wanted to hit me up with their apologies and say "I never meant to hurt you", but I wasn't trying to hear any of it. It had been a few weeks since our fight had popped off and my guess was it had finally hit both of them that I was an asset in both of their lives.

Nonetheless, I had gotten use to sex on a regular, so I was tempted to pick up the phone when Marshon called for the third time. I looked at my phone looking at his picture, and thought about the way he put it down and I had to toss my phone to prevent me from answering it.

I just couldn't go back to Marshon, could I? Shaking that thought I walked over to my closet looking for something that would get attention. Despite the fact that normally I was a relationship type of person, I really was horny and feeling like the nigga with the right swag could get it. Damn I was starting to become someone different, but in my defense, I was feeling alone. After all, everyone that I had trusted had turned their backs on me. I just needed an outlet. I was too broke to be a shopper, so in my hood, it was either sex or dope, and I knew that I could never do dope.

I picked out a pair of red leggings and a maxi dress that stopped just under my ass. My heels were about four inches and every curve was poking out. I didn't know who I would meet, but I just needed him to say the right things. I was getting turned on with just the thought of releasing the frustration that had been building up.

I stood in my full mirror smoothing down my dress and looking at my reflection. Why I had to talk myself into going to the club, I will never know. I just knew that if I stayed home it was a good chance I would end up in Marshon's bed and that couldn't happen tonight. I grabbed my keys, my purse and a few condoms out of the night stand, just in case. I was determined to make my night out all about me and my needs. Life was too short to sit around in pity, so I was going to turn up!

Kre

It was the first weekend of May, my 16th birthday, and I was hype. The weather was real nice, so

Keon had put the rims back onto his BMW after they had been sitting in the apartment all winter. I was in the passenger seat, Monique was in the back, and Keon was speeding down Spring Garden St. on the way to a club called "Statuz." We were listening to Jay-Z, as usual.

Wes was going to meet us at the club, since he had to take care of some business first. Monique had an upset look on her face and she wasn't saying shit to either one of us. I figured she was upset that my brother had made her sit in the back and let me ride shotgun. I didn't care though; I was convinced that the night was going to be perfect.

When we parked up outside in the parking lot and chilled in the car, I could already hear the music coming from inside. I couldn't tell what the song was but I was already nodding to the beat. All I wanted to do was get inside and finally experience the club atmosphere for myself. We were supposed to wait outside for Wes, but I couldn't take the anticipation anymore. I could see a bunch of girls strolling up the steps that led to the front door and all of them had on super tight jean shorts with cut off shirts and looked good as hell. I had to be inside with them. I had been waiting my whole life for this!

Keon opened the glove compartment and took his gun from off of his hip. He tucked the burner underneath his paperwork and told me to do the same thing. It was the first time I saw Keon leave his gun in the car. No matter how much you tipped a bouncer or who you knew at the front door, you couldn't take your gun into the club. Nobody could; it was just the way that it was. Inside the club, if there was a conflict it had to get settled the old fashioned way; with fists. I hoped that wouldn't happen though, since I was younger and smaller than most of the dudes walking into the club.

Keon led the way to the front door and Monique followed behind me. Keon paid for all of us then the bouncers patted us down. They didn't bother to ask for I.D.; everybody knew who Keon was. Since I was with him, I was good too. Keon and Monique got neon-yellow wristbands since they were over 21. The wristbands let the bartenders know who could get served liquor and who couldn't. I thought about asking Keon to get me one, but I didn't want to push it. I was just excited to finally be in the building with my big brother.

Monique went right to the bar and got herself some colorful looking drink. I think it was called a Blue Motorcycle. Even with the alcohol in her hand, Monique still looked upset. I never saw her drink liquor before; I guess she was just stressed out. Living the life she did, I could understand why. Things were always moving at 100 mph in our worlds; it was part of being a true hustler.

Keon made a few rounds through the club before heading over to the bar. He took the time to introduce me to like 20 different people. There was no way I could remember all of their names but I shook their hands and they all wished me happy birthday. Just like us, most of them were hustlers too. I could tell just from the way they carried themselves. I even recognized some of them from our hood, but they looked way different in the club. In the streets, they were grimey niggas, but under the spotlight of the club they got their shine on.

I didn't want to be up under Keon all night, but I was afraid to leave his side because I didn't exactly know what to do. All the girls looked older than me, so I was a little intimidated to go and talk to any of them.

The DJ was playing some hot shit, but I wasn't about to start dancing since nobody else really was yet. I decided to just watch everybody and study how different types of people acted in the club. It was easy to tell who was getting money and who wasn't. The niggas with real paper were buying bottles, while the broke niggas brought drinks in plastic cups. All the broke bitches asked niggas to buy them drinks, while the classy women with their own paper waited for a nigga to offer them a drink. Only the real loser broads brought their own drinks; they were just hopeless.

Just as I was getting a little restless, I felt somebody come up from behind me and tap my shoulder.

"What's up? Remember me?" she said, as I turned around.

The girl looked real familiar, but I didn't know exactly where I knew her from.

"It's me, Kalihia. From West Park, on the 3rd floor." she said, acting like I was supposed to remember her.

I could never remember this girl never saying a word to me the whole time we were living in the projects together or going to school together. Now that I had dropped out, I guess I was more popular than when I was enrolled. That was some crazy shit. Finally, after looking Kalihia up and down I managed to speak.

"Oh, what's up? How you been?" I said.

"Good, just can't wait to be finished with school in a few weeks." she said.

"Ain't you a little young to be in here?" she asked me.

"Money don't have no age." I said back with a smile.

Kalihia laughed and then started asking me all these questions about what I was doing now. I treated her like a cop though; I only told her the bare minimum, I didn't get into any details about all the shit that I had been up to.

Even though I wasn't telling her shit about my life, Kalihia could tell I had grown up and I wasn't surprised. After all, I was at the bar, fresh in Armani and Gucci, with a bunch of money in my pocket. Kalihia wasn't naïve; she knew I was definitely involved in the game on some level or another. Where we were from, it seemed like that was the only way young niggas ever made money. In reality, I could have dropped out of school and had a full time job bagging groceries, but we both knew better than that. I was a hustler, and girls in Philly loved hustlers.

"So is your girlfriend in here with you tonight?" asked Kalihia.

"I don't have a girlfriend. Where's your man at?" I asked.

I vaguely remembered Kalihia used to go out with some bul from our building named Marshon. He was like 6'5 and supposed to be headed to college to play basketball. Other than that, I barely knew anything about the nigga.

"What? I don't fuck with that boy no more. I thought you knew." said Kalihia, with a funny look on her face.

My life was way too busy to keep up with who was dating who at my old high school so I had no idea

Kalihia and Marshon weren't together anymore and I really didn't care. At the moment I was focused on Kalihia's juicy ass thighs. She had on some black leggings and was looking thick as hell. I kept making small talk with her, but all I was thinking about was those thighs and that ass the whole time.

Kalihia

So I finally had this nigga Kre's attention! With these leggings on, I had a bunch of niggas attention, but Kre was the one I wanted. He was the youngest nigga in the building, and one of the sexiest in my opinion. I was sitting at the table alone despite the fact that three men had already bought me drinks and were clearly ready to see if I would give them a chance. However none of them really did it for me. I knew the man that I was going to end up fucking was going to have to come with it. I didn't want a fairy tale like Rhonda had said, but I did want that nigga you could look at and know he was going to send chills down my spine. I damn sure wasn't expecting to see Kre, but after looking at him, I knew my search was over.

Kre was looking good as hell, but best of all, finally he was looking at me. He wasn't the only nigga looking at me, but he was the one I wanted. I knew he was the youngest of them all, but in my eyes he had the brightest future. The truth was, I had always been crushing on Kre, but because he was younger, I fucked with Marshon. I secretly hoped that one day Kre would step to me, but he never did. Now was my chance to show him why I wasn't a waste of time, and I was the girl he needed.

I ran my hand over his letting him know that I really wanted to get to know him. He didn't pull back so I stepped into his space. He grinned and his smile stole my heart. I turned, wrapping his arms around my waist so he could get a closer look at my ass that was now resting on his dick. I could feel it rise, but I didn't want to appear too easy so I pulled away and sat on the stool at the table.

I really didn't know what to say so I downed the rest of my drink and licked my lips seductively hoping that he would be buy me another one. Kre looked me up and down.

"What?" I asked sucking on a piece of ice, like it was his dick.

I couldn't tell if Kre and I were on the same page, I just knew that he was still there and I wasn't letting him out my sight, at least not until I got what I wanted. I wasn't a whore or anything, but I had needs. I wanted to feel like I could give myself to someone and know that they wouldn't fuck with my emotions. Kre was young, and I knew that he would be into me. I could mold him into my perfect man if I had to, but it was all going to start right in the club that we were in.

Kre

Keon grabbed a bottle of Moet, and then disappeared into a crowd of broads. He was pouring them up drinks so they were all on his dick. I recognized one of them from coming by the apartment the last time Monique went out of town. I knew Monique wouldn't like the way those hoes were all over Keon, but she was nowhere in sight so everything was cool for time being. After scanning the crowd for a minute I focused my attention back on Kalihia.

"So do you be comin' here a lot?" I asked.

"No not really. I'm just really stressed out so I needed to get out this weekend." said Kalihia.

I really couldn't think of much else to say to Kalihia but I didn't want to end our conversation. The problem was that we just didn't have much in common. I was into guns, money, and crack and unless Kalihia knew about shit like that I didn't know what else to say to her. Luckily, since I was at a loss for words Kalihia kept talking. Most of what she was saying went in one ear and out the other, but one question finally grabbed my attention.

"So do you wanna walk me outside?" asked Kalihia.

I didn't know exactly why Kalihia wanted me to walk her out the club, but she had a look in her eyes that told me she was feeling me. She just kept looking me up and down, biting on her bottom lip. "I'll walk you outside, just let me holla at my brother first." I said.

I pushed my way through the crowd by the bar and over toward where Keon was. By the time I got over there, Keon was already on his third bottle of Moet and was just about drunk.

"Kre what up! You enjoyin yourself?" asked Keon.

"Yeah, this shit is poppin'." I said.

"I wish my nigga Wes would hurry up and get here." said Keon, disappointed that his best friend wasn't right by his side poppin' bottles with him.

"Yo what's up with Monique? She looks like she's mad." I asked.

"She's cool. Women get like that sometime." said Keon.

Keon gave me that look that let me know it was one of those things I'd understand when I got a little older.

"Yo, this jawn want me to walk her outside." I said, as I pointed outKalihia.

"Damn, she thick as shit! I see we got the same taste in bitches. Must run in the family." said Keon.

After getting Keon's approval I headed back over to Kalihia. Some lame ass oldhead with a Rocawear tee shirt was buying her a drink, but I didn't care. I grabbed her arm gently, but still forcefully and led her out the front door. I had learned from watching my brother that women liked when a man took charge.

Soon as we stepped outside, I looked across the parking lot and saw Wes. He was standing beside his truck, talking on the phone and didn't even notice me. I wondered why he wasn't inside and I wanted to holla at him but I was more concerned with thick ass Kalihia at the moment. I never remembered her thighs or ass being so big before but then again she never wore tights to school.

⍰ Kalihia walked me over toward her car, which was parked toward the back of the lot. It was a squatter, an old ass Mazda 626 with fucked up paint and a doughnut. I tried not to laugh at her whip as we got inside, but I couldn't help it.

"It was so loud in the club, I just wanted to come outside so we could talk a little more." said Kalihia.

"What you wanna talk about?" I asked.

"Well I just wanted to tell you that I always thought you was cute. I used to like how you looked out for your little sister in school. And I like how you ain't disrespectful toward women like most boys be. So what do you think about me?" said Kalihia.

"I think you sexy and I dig your swag." I said.

Kalihia smiled and laughed.

"Good answer." she said.

As Kalihia kept giggling I looked out the car window toward Wes' truck. He was still standing there, but now he had company. He was talking with a man I had never seen before in my life. I knew that I had never seen him before because I would have definitely remembered a face like his. The man had long dreadlocks and a tattooed teardrop under his right eye. He was light-skinned and had a tattoo on his neck that said C-M-D so I guessed he was from Camden, NJ. He had a crazy look about him.

The man was wearing an all-white 10-Deep sweat suit, with white Adidas Shelltoes. He was listening close to every word that Wes said. I could tell they were talking about something really important.

"Come here." said Kalihia, as I finally stopped staring at Wes and the crazy looking man.

I was so focused on what was going on with Wes I hadn't even noticed that Kalihia had crawled into the backseat of her car. She had kicked off her shoes and was looking real relaxed. Just like she had told me to, I got into the backseat with her.

Kalihia smiled and then reached over and grabbed my dick. I didn't know what to say so I just sat still for a minute.

"You ain't scared are you?" asked Kalihia.

I was out in the street every day, toting my gun and enough cocaine to put me in prison for years. I had seen Bone get shot up, and even watched a nigga fall 19 stories off the top of the projects to his death. But for some reason, I was a little scared of Kalihia. She was two years older than me and I know she was more sexually experienced. The few girls that I had fucked were my own age, and on my level sexually. Kalihia was different though; she was like a grown woman. That was intimidating to me.

□ Kalihia straddled herself across me and kissed my lips. She slid her tights down to her ankles and I did the same thing with my jeans.

"You got a condom?" she asked.

"No." I answered.

"It's cool, I got some." said Kalihia.

She reached into her handbag and grabbed out a box of Trojan condoms. She handed me the rubber and I slipped it on. After that, it was on and poppin.'Kalihia bounced up and down on my dick like she was on a trampoline. I really didn't even have to do anything, except enjoy it. She kept rotating her hips and squeezing her thigh muscles which felt incredible. It didn't take long before Kalihia had me ready to bust. My brain was whispering for me to hold back the nut, but my dick was screaming to let it loose. So I did.

⍰ Kalihia wasn't even mad that I had came kind of quick, she just got off from on top of me and pulled her tights back up.

"You goin' back inside the club?" she asked me.

"Yeah." I said.

"Ok, well let's exchange numbers so we can stay in touch. Call me when you leave tonight, OK?" she said.

"All right then." I replied.

I called Kalihia's number, then saved it in my phone and hopped out her little squatter. She had obviously got what she had come out of the house for, so she was headed home for the night. I was anxious to get back inside and tell my brother what had just happened. I was so hype I forgot all about Wes and the crazy looking nigga he had been talking to, until I saw them out the corner of my eye. I noticed Wes was handing the man some cash. I thought maybe he was a new connect that Wes and Keon fucked with that I didn't know. As I thought about everything, I heard Keon calling me. He had made his way out of the club.

"Kre! What's up playboy? Come here." hollered Keon, from all the way across the parking lot.

Keon was drunk and had what seemed like every woman who had been in the club around him; except for Monique. I didn't know where she was. I walked up to Keon and shook his hand. Before I could even tell him about knocking off Kalihia, Keon started speaking.

"Fuck this club! Yo, I'm bout to rent out a suite at the Mariott for the night. We gonna turn this into a hotel party!" said Keon.

Keon was trippin' though; I knew Monique wasn't going for all that. I started to tell Keon to fall back, but I never even got a chance to get the words out of my mouth. Before I could even blink, bullets started flying in our direction! The crowd stared scrambling to get out of the way as the slugs went everywhere.

I was looking at my brother to see what I should do since Keon always knew what to do in crazy situations. But this time, Keon couldn't help me. Three bullets had hit Keon; all of them headshots.

"Shit!" I screamed out, as I got even closer to my brother.

Keon was lying on the ground, not moving at all. Blood was everywhere. Then, I felt a pain like I had never felt before. My body felt like it was on fire. I wanted to get up off the cement, but I couldn't move. I had been shot too!

Chapter 6

Kalihia

After the club, I went and grabbed a chicken cheesesteak with fries and then walked down South Street by myself for a little while. Being out all alone was strange, but it was just what I needed. Sometimes, a woman has to be her own best friend. Kre hadn't called my phone, which was pissing me off because I knew for a fact that the club had let out already.

"Niggas ain't shit." I mumbled to myself, as I double checked my call log and made sure my ringer was turned on.

I had given this nigga all this good pussy for free and all I asked him to do was one simple thing; call me when he left the club. His little young ass couldn't even do that! Who the fuck did this youngbul think he was?

Frustrated, I stepped into Wawa and grabbed an Apple Snapple when I heard two people in front of me talking loudly. I was annoyed that they were so loud, but then I heard Keon's name and the word 'dead' followed behind it. I moved closer to make sure that I heard clearly.

"Hell yeah that nigga got three in the dome, nigga." one of the boys said, and I couldn't help but to intrude.

"You talkin' about Keon Carter?" I questioned, thinking about Kre.

"Yeah, the bul from West Park. He got killed tonight." one of the men confirmed.

It was bugging me out that Kre didn't call me, but now I was starting to understand. Kre was dealing with the loss of his brother. I was feeling bad about being mad at Kre when he was obviously going through hell. Then, the reality hit me that I could have gotten shot if I had stayed at Statuz a little longer.

I stood spaced out for a minute thinking about my life. I loved the club life, but I had no plans on dying in one. I had to make smarter choices. I realized that in just an instant shit can change up like that. The phrase 'here today, gone tomorrow' took on a whole new meaning to me at that moment.

"You buying that or not, Ma?" the cashier asked, snapping me out of my trance.

"Yeah." I said, as I put my juice up on the counter, then paid and walked out the store.

I was walking as fast as I could, but didn't really have a destination. My car was parked on a side block, so I figured I would head towards it. At that point, I guessed that heading home was my only option. After all the music stopped playing and the drinks stopped flowing, I was still dealing the reality that I lived with my drug addict of a mother in the damn 'jects. At least I was living though; it was a shame I couldn't say the same for poor Keon.

I couldn't imagine what him and his family were going through.

"Here today and gone tomorrow," kept echoing through my head, as I tried desperately to collect my thoughts.

It was a damn shame, but that's how things worked in our hood. Life wasn't promised, the streets were crazy as hell. They didn't call it Killadelphia, Pistolvania for nothing!

Kre

My brother was gone and I wasn't dealing with that shit too well at all. Keon was like my hero; he was a black Superman to me. How the fuck do you kill Superman? The whole situation was just unreal. Life as I knew it was forever changed. The pain was too much to deal with, but I had no choice except to accept it.

During the melee, I had taken a shot to the hip, but luckily the bullet just grazed me. My thigh was hurt and I was limping a little bit, but I was alright for the most part. My mom was absolutely distraught; her oldest child was dead. No parent should have to bury their own seed, but that was exactly what she was being forced to do. I was back at her apartment in the projects recuperating and doing my best to comfort her and Kenya, but it was difficult for all of us.

"Damn, this funeral home wants way more money than I got," Mom cried out, after getting off the phone with the funeral director.

My mom was upset that there wasn't enough money to send Keon off in style. She knew that her son was always a flashy bul and would have wanted a memorable funeral, but she simply couldn't afford it. Mom just didn't have any money, but I knew back at our apartment Keon's safe contained some cash that could solve that problem. My brother hadn't grinded hard for the past five years to be put in a cheap pine box.

I decided to call up Monique and let her know that I would be dropping by the apartment as soon as I found a ride. It was tacky to be calling her up and talking about money, but there were issues that needed to be taken care of and Monique had the combo to the safe. The towing company had impounded Keon's

Beamer since he obviously couldn't drive it home from the club. I would be damned if I let Philadelphia Parking Authority end up auctioning off my brother's whip because we left it sitting on the lot collecting fees. That car was Keon's pride and joy so I had to go pay the parking authority and go get that.

"This is Mo. I'm not available right now. Leave me one and I'll hit you back." was all I heard when I dialed Monique's phone.

My call went straight to voicemail, which was frustrating. I figured I would give Monique a little while before I called again, because she was probably fucked up over losing her boyfriend. After all, she had been with Keon for a few years. She was close to him too, so she had to be hurting.

"Answer the door Kenya!" Mom hollered out.

She had gotten sick of people coming by to offer condolences for Keon. They were dropping off all types of grieving food, but she needed cash. Fuck all the hams, chicken, and baked pies; she wanted money! However, the person at the door wasn't bringing by any food.

"Is Kre here?" I heard a female voice ask, as my sister stood in the doorway.

It took me a second, but I pegged the voice to Kaihlia, the jawn I had smashed outside the club the night before.

"Yeah, I'm here. Come in," I said, speaking up for myself.

Kenya let Kailhia in and after she offered some condolences to her and my Mom, Kaihlia walked over to where I was laying on the couch. I looked at her and for the first time all day I cracked a smile. She was wearing some more leggings, similar to the ones from the club but this time they were grey. It hadn't been a fluke; Kaihlia was definitely thick as hell. She had a long button down Aeri shirt covering her donk, but she couldn't hide that wagon no matter how hard she tried.

"I just heard about your brother. I'm sorry for your loss," Kaihlia said.

"Thanks," I dully replied.

It wasn't that I didn't appreciate Kaihlia's sympathy; it was just that none of that was going to bring my brother back.

"Is there anything I can do to help you or your family?" she asked.

"Actually there is."

Kaihlia sat down on the couch and crossed her wide legs.

"Just let me know what you need," she said in a sincere voice.

"Can you give me a ride over to my brother's apartment?" I asked.

"Sure baby. Are you ready now?" asked Kaihlia.

Wow; I was her 'baby' now. I didn't know how we had gotten to that stage after a quick car fuck outside of a nightclub, but I guess I was cool with it. Kaihlia damn sure was the sexiest girl I had ever been with. Matter of fact, she was the sexiest *woman* I had ever been with. Kaihlia was definitely grown as opposed to the other females that I had dealt with.

I slipped on one of my old outfits that I had left at my Mom's apartment; an old orange Sean John shirt and some no-name jeans. I would never wear that type of bullshit anymore, but all my clothes were also at the apartment. Keon had upgraded me from a sloppy ass dresser to a fresh little nigga, but at the moment being fresh and stylish was the last thing on my mind. The other reason I needed to get to the apartment was that besides Keon's safe money, I also had my sock stash underneath the air mattress.

Kaihlia led the way to her little squatter and after a few attempts, the hoopty started up. It sounded it terrible, but it got us across town and to the apartment successfully. I still had my key to the spot so I led the way inside.

"Monique! You here?" I hollered as I let myself in.

However, there was no reply. I clicked on the light and looked around the apartment. If Monique wasn't home, I still wouldn't be able to get Keon's money from the safe, which had me upset all over again. Just when I thought I was solving problems, I was back to square one.

"Damn it!" I said, walking into Monique and Keon's bedroom.

I went into Keon's closet, looking at all his fly ass clothes and reminiscing on my brother for a second. I was thinking about how much I was going to miss him when I turned my attention to the bottom of the closet, where the safe was. To my surprise, the safe was open!

I swung the small safe door all the way open as Kaihlia looked over my shoulder. However, the safe was completely empty. It was bone dry, like the Mohave Desert! My brother's stash was gone. My mind started working quickly as I added everything up. Monique was the only person besides Keon who knew the combo to the safe. Keon was dead and she was nowhere to be found. All the money was gone. It didn't take a fool to see that something wasn't right!

I darted from out of my brother's bedroom and over to mine. I flipped up my air mattress and found my sock stash. Luckily, that was intact. However, I only had a few racks. I obviously wasn't getting money like my brother was. As Kaihlia looked on, I stormed through the house like a madman. Next, I made my way to the bathroom. Underneath the sink was where Keon kept crack that hadn't been bagged up yet. Just like I figured, there were 4 and a half ounces and a scale sitting under the sink.

I was in a panic mode, but I instructed Kaihlia to take the work and tuck it under one of my shirts and put it in her car. Then I ransacked the apartment for some clothes, my little stash sock, and the Playstation and headed out. Something was definitely up. I could tell now that Keon's death was more than just some random club shooting. I didn't have everything figured out, but I knew one thing; Monique was living foul. My brother was dead and she thought that she was just going to take his hard earned money and disappear. Nah, fuck that! I wasn't going to allow that to happen. I owed that much to my brother.

"I gotta figure this shit out!" I mumbled to my brother, as I grabbed my stuff and headed out to Kaihlia's car.

Kalihia

I sat in my car face to face with Kre. He had been through so much this week and I felt as if there was something I needed to say. I really was unsure how to approach the whole situation. For him to lose your brother and then find out his girl robbed him, was not set up in my favor. I had been waiting for this nigga to give me the time of day and in one moment another bitch could have already blown it for me. Getting him to trust in me and believe that I wasn't out to get him was not going to be easy.

"So, how much did she take?" I asked him with a frown on my face.

"What does that matter?" Kre yelled, and I knew that shit was going from bad to worse.

I grabbed his hand and cupped it with mine.

"Damn Kre, I'm asking so that I know how much we got to make back."

Kre opened his mouth and I felt as if I could read his mind before he spoke, so I cut him off.

"Look Kre, fuck her. She was grimy from the start and not ready to be with a boss nigga like Keon, but I ain't her. I know you a boss and I'm ready to help you build." I told him.

He pulled away from me and scratched his head. I was holding my breath, worried about what he might say, but in that moment, if he didn't believe the truths I was telling he didn't deserve me.

"Man, I ain't really trying to hear that shit," he said to me.

I was thinking to myself '*Fuck it, I don't even care*,"

However, I did care and tears ran down my face as I started my car. I wiped my face and started to drive. Not wanting to look at Kre, I turned up my radio and just blasted whatever song was playing. Music couldn't help me escape the emotions that I was feeling.

After a short, but tense and awkward drive, we pulled up in front of our building and I just cut the car off and sat there. The music was still playing, but for once that wasn't working, and the awkward silence between us was speaking loud and clear.

"Kre I told you how I feel, is that not enough!" I was yelling and smacking my hands together like one of those hood dudes when they get mad.

"You think I fuck every nigga the first night, because I don't, you..."

Kre grabbed me and started kissing my lips, I'm sure it was to shut me up, but at this point I didn't care. I crawled on top of his lap and continued to kiss him. We finally came up for air, so I rested my head on his shoulder and just rested there like we were in the bed.

"Damn babe you thick as hell," Kre said as I kissed his neck some more.

"Ok," I told him kissing on him.

"That's a nice way of saying yo fat ass killing my legs," he joked, kissing me again, before I climbed back onto my side of the car.

We stared at each other a little longer, before I realized it was after midnight.

"Babe I have to work in the morning, so can we hook up after I get off?" I asked and he just nodded while opening the door.

We both got out the car, and walked towards the stair way.

"You want me to walk you up?" Kre asked as I grabbed his hand.

"What you about to do?" I asked looking at him look and the crowd of niggas smoking.

"Go ahead, I will be good," he assured me.

We kissed one last time and I watched him walk off as I climbed all the flights of stairs. As I was walking my phone began to buzz and I paused on the stair way reading a text from Kre telling me to text him, when I'm in the bed.

"I knew I had made the right choice. Kre was so different from Marshon, and the whole time I was with Kre I stayed smiling even though we were mostly talking about real serious shit.

"Where you been?" I heard a voice ask, and I thought I was losing my mind.

I looked up from my phone and saw Marshon sitting on the stairs, right before my floor.

"Don't you stay on the eighth floor?" I asked, walking towards my apartment, trying to ignore him, but for some reason he feels as if he needs to follow.

"Where you been?" Marshon asked again, as I took my keys out and opened my door letting myself in.

"Yo, I can't come in?" he asked and I smirked.

"For what Shon, I don't think my man would like that," I said feeling good watching his face flip upside down realizing that I had a man.

I started to close the door in Marshon's face and he put his foot in inching his way in. I rolled my eyes and stepped aside allowing him in. I locked the door and followed him to my bedroom. He made himself comfortable on my bed, and I started to feel annoyed.

I texted Kre letting him know I was in the house, and I sat down beside Marshon to see what he felt he needed to talk about.

"So whats up?" I asked Marshon.

"You trying to make me mad, saying you got a man. That shit is real funny."

"Nigga I'm not trying to make you mad. Kre is my man!" I told him, pissed that he felt like I had to lie to him.

I would never stoop to his level.

"Wait, the little nigga from, down stairs? That's who was with til' damn near one in the morning?" he asked, laughing under his breath.

"Yeah his brother just got killed, he needed me to do some things for him. So I did." I explained.

"Shit my brother got smoked and you don't hear me being a little bitch about it," loudly replied Marshon.

"Kre wasn't being a little bitch," I said, pausing when I realized what he had said.

"Your brother died?" I asked feeling sorry that we had been fighting.

"Hell yeah, that's why that nigga hasn't been coming around in the past few months. My mom is stressing, on top of that money is getting' light." he told me, causing me to really feel bad.

I really didn't know how to react, so I just sat still.

"Yeah, but you don't see me whining," Marshon said, laying back on my bed.

I really didn't know what to say so I just lied beside him. I had so much on my mind and I just need to relax. Besides all the shit with Kre, my mom was back to her old ways running the streets and God knows where she was at. All I could do was pray for her safety, as I laid down across my bed. Marshon was hurt about his brother, even though he was trying not to show it.

*****

Before I knew it my phone was buzzing and it was nine in the morning! I woke up next to Marshon holding me tightly. I grabbed my phone looking at a text from Kre, He thanked me for being there for him last night, and I looked back at Marshon feeling like every word that I had said to Kre was a lie.

Why did love and relationships always have to be so hard? I wanted my heart to be all the way in with Kre, but I couldn't deny my feelings for Marshon. We had history and I couldn't ignore that. Kre was definitely on my mind, but as I looked over at Marshon, the love was still there. He had done me dirty with the whole Rhonda situation, but I knew that sometimes niggas thought with their dicks and not their hearts. I was torn and my thoughts weren't giving me a clear answer as to what to do next.

Chapter 7

Kre

Everything was out of order in my life but the one good thing I had going for me was Kalihia. She was acting like she was really down for a nigga and truly had my back. I had to respect that and I appreciated it because if I was going to make things better for my family, I was going to need her help. I had left that four and a half ounces in her car since my Mom didn't allow for any drug related shit to go on at her crib. West Park was public housing and any drug charges would get us kicked out of there. If we lost that apartment, my family would be all the way fucked up.

My plan was to go and holla at Wes with the drugs that I had. Wes was a hustler with plenty of customers so I was sure that he would buy the work from me. Then, with that money, we would at least have enough to give the funeral director a down payment. After that, I could see about tracking down my brother's BMW. First, I needed to holla at Kalihia though. I would need her to drive me over to Wes' spot and talk to him about the moves I was trying to make and also to tell him about the grimey shit Monique had done.

I slipped on some of Keon's old Gucci rubber slides and my Adidas ball shorts with a hoodie and headed for Kalihia's apartment. Having a girl that lived in the same building was convenient as hell, I thought as I knocked on her door. To my surprise though, Kalihia was not the one who opened up the door.

"Yizzo, what's up lil' nigga?" said Marshon, as he opened the door drinking a big ass glass of orange Kool-Aid.

"What's up?" I mumbled back.

"Everything good with you?" he asked, smirking.

"I'm straight." I said.

"All right den." said Marshon, as he put his hand on top of my head and palmed my scalp like I was a youngbul.

I just looked this tall nigga up and down as he stood in the doorway. Why the fuck was he in her apartment at 9 A.M.? He damn sure hadn't stopped by to borrow some sugar from Kalihia's mother!

"Hit my phone later, Kalihia." Marshon said, as he brushed past me and strolled cockily out of the apartment.

Kalihia sashayed her thick ass to the door, still in her night clothes which consisted of some Aerie boy shorts and a wife beater. She was coming from the bathroom doing that little stank walk that Monique would do every morning after her and my brother had sex all night. I just stood there calmly, refusing to show any type of jealousy. I was too cool for all that.

"Kre, I can explain. It ain't what it looks like..." started Kalihia.

I wasn't interested in hearing her cop any pleas thought. It was what it was. She wasn't officially my girl, so she was free to do whatever she wanted.

"Explain what?" I sarcastically replied.

"Don't be like that. Marshon came over to talk and we fell asleep. He's going through some family stuff too," Kalihia said, as she motioned for me to come inside the apartment.

"Oh, I ain't trippin' off that. But yo, I need a lil' favor." I said.

"Sure, baby. Just tell me what you need me to do."

At first, I was going to ask Kalihia to ride me over to Wes' apartment up near City Line Ave, but after seeing Marshon leave out of her place, I felt some type of way. I really wasn't even in the mood to be around her.

"I need to borrow your car real quick." I said.

"Ok, do you want me to come with you?" she asked.

"Nah, I'm good. It will only take me like an hour at the most."

"All right, cause I gotta go to work today. And I may need to go searching for my Mom, she didn't come home last night." said Kalihia, as she handed me the keys.

I didn't even bother to say thanks; I just took the keys and bolted for the steps.

"These hoes is somethin' else." I mumbled to myself.

*****

Kaihlia's little squatter ran like a piece of shit. I would have been better off riding a bicycle! She needed a tune up, an oil change and a timing belt. It was like the harder I mashed the gas, the slower the car went.

"Damn!" I screamed in frustration, as I could hardly get up enough speed to change lanes.

I had work in the car, so I wasn't trying to be dilly-dalling out in traffic. I wanted to get to Wes' spot, do what I had to do and get back to the hood. Unfortunately, the Philadelphia morning rush hour traffic was making that pretty damn difficult. See, in

Philly traffic, putting on a turn signal and waiting patiently until someone let you in would get a driver nowhere fast. Instead, I had to broadie my way into the next lane.

I whipped my wheel to the left and cut off an oncoming Ford Fusion. I got the finger and a few curse words from the pissed off driver, but I didn't really give a fuck about his feelings. What I did give a fuck about was the police car that had witnessed my little move.

"Shit. I know he ain't 'bout to pull me over!" I said, as the cop accelerated and got behind me.

Like always, I hadn't seen the cop sitting there until it was too late. Now, this muthfacka was behind me with his lights on. I was fucked. I didn't have a piece of a license, no insurance, and I didn't even know if Kaihlia's car was registered. On top of all that, I was riding dirty with the four and a half ounces!

I weighed my options real quick and decided that pulling over wasn't one! I had try and shake the cops off of my tail. Had I been in Keon's Beamer with the V8, I would have easily toasted the cop. In Kaihlia's P.O.S., it was going to be a challenge. First, I put the blinker on and edged to the side of the road. The cop pulled behind me and after a few seconds, he opened his door and proceeded towards the car. That was my chance to bounce. By the time he got back inside his car, I would have a nice head start on him, I figured.

I flipped the squatter back into drive and took off! I jumped right back into the flow of traffic and floored it. Looking in my rearview, I could see the policeman radioing for backup, so I knew it was about to go down. He wasn't just going to let me get away without giving chase.

I knew that I needed to try and lose the cop, so I took the first right turn that I saw. Riding around with Monique had taught me all the shortcuts in the city, and even if I didn't know exactly where I was at, I had a general idea of my direction. I made another left turn to further confuse the cop and before I knew it, I was on a small side block.

"I gotta ditch this car, he probably ran the plates." I said out loud.

Quickly, I grabbed my drugs, my phone and left Monique's car parked on the side of the road. I was on foot now, so in a way that gave me an advantage. I dipped up the first alleyway that I saw and was quickly on the next block. Even if the cop saw me, there was no way that he could prove I had been the one driving the car.

With the work still tucked into the shirt, I played it cool. I looked like a regular kid walking the street. I even stopped off at the bodega and brought a Snapple and some chips. I really just used the plastic grocery bag to stash my work in though. I had a long walk ahead of me, but I had to get to Wes' house. Shit was getting real crazy.

*****

I knew Kaihlia was going to be mad, so I didn't even bother to respond to her text and let her know that I was going to be back with her car. Shit, I wasn't going to be able to bring her car back at all. I had to abandon that shit on the side of the road. Most likely, once the police found it they were going to toe it. I would have to make it up to her at some point, but at the moment my current focus was on getting to Wes. Wes was my brother's right hand man, and Keon always told me that I could count on him in tough situations. This was a tough situation.

I figured that Wes was probably fucked up over Keon's death just like me since they were so close. He hadn't come by my Mom's apartment which was kind of weird, but everyone has their own way of grieving so I couldn't be mad at him. I just wanted to get Wes to take the four and a baby off of my hands and put some cash in my pocket. I needed a few racks to get things back in order, and I knew that Wes was a hustler. I wasn't asking him for any favors, so I figured things would go smooth.

After walking damn near 30 blocks, which took me forever, I was finally on Wes' street. The small bullet wound in my hip had been aggravated from all the walking, but I dealt with it. Physically, I was beat and the Gucci slides that I had chosen to wear were damn near ruined. If Keon was alive, he would be pissed that I fucked up his $200 slippers running through the streets, I thought.

I walked up on Wes' crib and even though I had only been there one time, I remembered the house. His black Tahoe sitting outside made me sure that I was at the right place. However, as I got closer to the crib I noticed another car pulling up in front of the house. I did a double take to be sure; it was Keon's BMW. I damn sure wasn't expecting to see my brother's car. At first I figured Wes had gone and gotten it out of the pound, but then I noticed that Wes was standing in his front door waiting for the car to pull up. I positioned myself where I could see him, but he couldn't see me. The BMW shut off, the door flung open, and out stepped Monique!

Monique was wearing her trademark, tight, hip-hugging, 7 For All Mankind jeans, some flats, and a button down shirt. She hopped out the car and sashayed over to Wes' front door, as I looked on confused as hell.

"Hey bae!" she said as Wes opened the door for her.

"What's up, baby?" said Wes, as he wrapped his arm around Monique's plump ass and palmed it with his hand.

Finally, Wes leaned down and tongue kissed Monique for a few seconds. The she stepped inside and Wes closed the door behind them. I was shocked, but I knew that something damn sure wasn't right about this situation! Wes and Monique were both living foul as hell.

Kalihia

I slipped on my gym shoes, put my heels in my book bag, and grabbed my keys, purse and phone from my bed. I looked at the time on my phone and was a little annoyed that Kre still was not back. He had come got my car hours ago, and still not returned. I had to be at work in the next hour, and really didn't have time to wait, I couldn't afford to miss a day of work nor did I want to lose my job. My only choice was SEPTA public transportation.

Walking to the bus stop, all I could think about was the look in Kre's eyes earlier in the morning.

Did he really not care that Marshon was at my house? Was I really just sex to him? Couldn't he see how much I really cared about him?

I looked up as the bus pulled in front of me and stepped inside. As I paid my fare, I noticed a familiar face that I didn't care to see sitting towards the back;

Rhonda! I scanned the bus for an empty seat so that I didn't have to sit anywhere near her. I found a seat towards the front, plopped down and looked out the window, sure not to make eye contact with the back stabbing bitch.

However, she noticed me and wanted to talk. The nerve of this thot!

"Hey," Rhonda said, walking over and sitting down next to me.

I looked in her direction briefly and returned my gaze back out the window.

"Kalihia, really? You gone sit there and act like you don't see or hear me?" Rhonda said, as I continued to ignore her.

"Look, I'm sorry but you know how I am. It just kind of happened. We were talking about how you was acting like the virgin Mary, and he had a game and just needed to bust a nut. I wasn't going to, and I didn't mean to let it get so far, but oh my God you know how Marshon is. He can be real persuasive when he starts rubbin' all the right places," Rhonda explained.

"Wow! Like did you really come over here to discuss sex with my ex with me?" I asked her, standing and walking to the other side of the bus.

I was trying my best to stay chill, but Rhonda was truly pissing me off and I really didn't know how much more of her mouth I could take.

"So almost ten years of friendship is over like that?" Rhonda asked looking at me with puppy dog eyes.

"You slept with my fuckin boyfriend! Did you want me to welcome you back in my life, like everything can ever be the same? How in the hell can I ever trust you?" I asked rolling my eyes at how dumb Rhonda sounded.

I dug into my pocket and pulled out my phone attached my ear buds and started to listen to Meek Mill blocking the sound of this annoying bitch's voice. Then she tugged my ear buds out of my ear and began to roll her neck!

"Bitch don't act all high and mighty! You knew I liked Marshon first," she said, like that made anything better.

I stood up, getting directly into her face.

"What you won't do is touch me or my shit again," I said, as I slipped my ear buds back in and sat down.

"So when he picked you I had to be ok, but when he wants me, you mad. I can't help it if my pussy is the best," she said.

I smiled at her comment.

"That's why he was in my bed last night," I said laughing.

I don't even know why I made a big deal of it, but the look on her face was priceless. Then Rhonda stepped in my face, and ripped my ear buds out tugging my phone to the floor. Before I knew it, I had grabbed her by her light brown weave and slung her into the seats across from of us. I bent to pick up my phone and felt her hands around my leg pulling me to the floor. We rolled around on the floor pulling each other's hair until someone pulled us apart and we were ordered off the bus. I grabbed my book bag and phone and jumped off the bus.

"Dumb bitch, you better watch your back." Rhonda said.

"I don't have to; Marshon has always done it." I said with a smile, walking up the street.

It was only a block or so to work so I walked the rest of the way. When I got to work I scrolled down my text and call log, and Kre had not even hit me up. I was disappointed to say the least. Going into the bathroom, I pulled out my brush, and pulled my hair into a pony tail. I then texted Kre, that I needed a ride home from work, around 10. I was hoping when he picked me up we could talk and he would finally allow me explain why Marshon was at my house.

*****

Hour after hour passed at work, and I heard nothing from Kre.

"This nigga better have a damn good excuse why he ain't texting me back. He is irkin me." I said, as I made sure the ringer on my phone was working properly.

Kre left me no choice. I was off of work and I had to get home. I didn't do SEPTA at night; too many crazy muthafuckas were on the bus by then. Regretfully, I looked through the contacts in my phone and scrolled down to the one person that I knew would come and get me; Marshon.

The boosters who supported the college teams that were interested in Marshon provided him with rental cars, so he stayed with transportation. It as illegal as hell, but college sports were a dirty business. I texted Marshon and right away, he hit me back informing me that he was on the way. As fucked up as the nigga was, I could still count on him for some things.

Before I knew it, Marshon was coming up the block. I stood outside my job watching, as he pulled up in a nice little SUV. Damn, I couldn't front, he was looking good with the driver seat leaned back, and his head bobbing to that Kendrick Lamar. I opened the door, praying to God Marshon didn't give me grief for having to call him at 11 at night. I had no other choice; Kre had my car and was ignoring every text I shot him.

"Where is your car?" Marshon asked as soon as I closed the door.

I looked away and put my seatbelt on, avoiding the question. Marshon smirked, then licked his sexy ass lips. I couldn't deny Marshon was looking good in his True Religion jeans, Pink Dolphin hoodie and matching snapback, but after all that he had put me through I was not trying to back track.

"What up ma, where is your lil' man at?" Marshon mockingly asked as we approached a red light.

His glance left the road and his eyes roamed my body.

"Look Shon, I'm tired so can we avoid the small talk?" I asked staring out the window.

I hated to admit the fact that I was wondering where the hell Kre was. I didn't know if I should be worried, or mad at this point and I wanted to cry.

"You don't want to talk about it, because you know it's not shit that young nigga can do with you. You been with a man, now you going to be with a kid? How is that going to work, Khailia?" Marshon asked, looking from me to the road.

I knew he was trying to piss me off so I chose to ignore his words, but he could tell they were getting to me. We pulled up in front of the building, and I reached for the door, however Marshon grabbed my face. He forced me to look in his eyes and I was more than annoyed.

"Let me go, Shon!"

"Come lay with me tonight, you know I miss you babe," he said, and I rolled my eyes.

His hand brushed my cheek, sending a chill down my spine.

"So, you don't miss me, baby?"

"Baby"; that's just what he had called Rhonda! I had almost gone for Marshon's bullshit, but I caught myself.

"Nope, I'm good," I told him, pulling away from his grasp.

As always though, Marshon was aggressive. He treated women the same way he treated basketball players and did whatever he wanted to do to them. Marshon pulled me back and placed his lips on mine. He was trying to force his tongue down my throat.

I drew back and smacked him. Finally, I ripped the door open and gave him an evil eye.

"I'm with Kre, Shon. You had me and didn't want me, and now you do. Boy, now that's some childish shit," I said.

"You with Kre, huh? Well answer me this; where is he at?"

That was the million dollar question. I hopped out of the truck and slammed the door, vanishing into the building. The whole time I was wondering just where was Kre with my car and why he hadn't texted or called me. Little did I know that he was going to have a hell of a story for me!

Chapter 8

Kre

I decided to hike it all the way back to the hood. Before my brother passed he had told me that cops were getting slick to niggas who tried to move work on the bus. He said that SEPTA had even gone as far as putting undercover officers on the buses, so I wasn't about to take that chance even though my hip was killing me. Cab drivers were reluctant to go my hood since a few of them had gotten robbed recently. So, I hoofed it all the way home.

I had abandoned Kaihlia's car and I was sure that it had been towed which had me kind of upset. Even though I was mad at her over seeing Marshon leave her apartment at 9 A.M., I still felt bad about it. In our hood, cars weren't easy to come by, especially for young people like Kaihlia. Now, she was assed out and that shit was all my fault. I was going to have to make it up to her, but I figured I could start with an apology.

I walked straight up to Kaihlia's door and knocked, not knowing who would answer this time. Luckily, it was her. Kaihlia had on some leggings and a baby tee with her hair wrapped up in a silk scarf for the night. She was looking at me and I could tell she was pissed off as hell.

"Well..." she said, waiting for me to explain why I hadn't bothered to bring her car back or even pick her up from work.

Dealing with an angry black woman in the middle of the night wasn't much fun at all.

"Look, I don't know how to tell you this but I got your car towed." I came right out and said.

I swore I saw steam shoot from Kaihlia's head at that moment.

"You did what nigga? That whip wasn't even in my name! Ain't no way I'm gonna be able to get that shit back. Ugh!" she hollered, loud enough for the whole hallway to hear.

I explained to Kaihlia about the cops pulling me over and how I tried to bounce, but she still was upset. I could understand why she was mad, but after the shit I had discovered about Monique and Wes I wasn't in the mood to hear it.

"Yo, just let me get my brother's body put in the fuckin' ground and then I'll pay you back for your damn car! Shit, if Wes wasn't so worried about fuckin' Monique I could have sold him the work and paid you by now." I screamed.

"Wait, Monique? Your brother's girl? She's fuckin' his best friend already? Damn." said Kaihlia, with sympathy in her voice.

"I saw her tongue the nigga down and go into his house today. But look, none of that matters. I'm in this shit alone now so I'm gonna do what I gotta do." I said, as I walked away.

"You ain't alone, Kre. Why come you can't realize that you got me?" Kaihlia pleaded.

"Whatever." I said, as I headed for the stairs that led back to my apartment, still clutching the bag with the work in it.

I was frustrated as hell, but I had to deal with all my issues. I needed to get some answers about what was going on with Monique and Wes. I figured that would put me on the path to getting everything straightened out. On the strength of my brother Keon, I had to be a man and fix all of this shit! Reluctantly, I hid the drugs under my bed and took a long, hot shower. I had some serious decisions to make, and soon.

Kalihia

Fuck, I couldn't win for losing. I really liked Kre and for him to come sit in my face after not coming to pick me up from work and say he lost my car knocked me off my rocker. Then, he sat there and said he's in this shit alone. What the fuck! My mom was on drugs, my best friend was fucking my ex, and my man had walked out on me. God knows all that had me crying again, sick of being in my damn feelings.

"Damn why shit like this always happen to me?" I said under my breath, still staring at the door that Kre had just walked out of.

I couldn't just continue to feel like this. Something had to give. I had to change something in my life, I thought as I walked into my bedroom and slipped on my sneakers. I just needed to vent, so I made my way up to the eighth floor. I stood in front of Marshon's door beyond nervous to knock. I kept looking behind me; for some reason I felt as if someone was following me. I know it was crazy to feel so paranoid, but with all that had been going on lately, I was.

I really didn't know why I was stressing, I had been with Marshon for a minute so I should have never needed a specific reason to go see him. However, after the blow up we'd just had in his car, I worried he might not even be talking to me. I tapped on the door and stood there with my hands shaking.

"Fuck this," I mumbled to myself, starting to walk away as the door opened.

"Yo, you not gonna come in?" Marshon asked.

I really wanted to continue to the stairs. However, Marshon had already seen me so the hard part was over.

"Didn't know if you were home," I told him walking back to the door.

Marshon took a step back and allowed me to enter. I stood in the tiny hall looking at Marshon. He was top less and his red Nike jogging pants hung off his ass showing the band of his boxer briefs. I had to cup my hands together to prevent touching the tattoo on his chest I always touched when we sexed.

"Can we talk?" I asked him watching as he closed the door and made his way to his bedroom. I followed, but the whole time I questioned if I should have been there.

"I knew ya little ass would miss me," Marshon said, closing his door and falling onto his bed.

I smirked and looked over to the window.

"So whats up baby?' Marshon said.

I just started to cry. He stood and pulled me backwards. He plopped back down on his bed this time with me on his lap. His lips fell on my neck and I wanted to pull away, but it felt good.

"Oh my God Shon, I feel like everything is going wrong, and I don't know how to fix it!" I told him, pulling myself to my feet and pacing the bedroom.

If I had a cigarette I would have fired it up.

"Come sit down," Marshon said, pulling me back over to him.

"No I can't, I feel so annoyed right now."

"Why what's going on?" Marshon said with compassion.

He stood wrapping his arms around my body. I sighed and let more tears fall.

"So today I let Kre borrow my car, and he got it towed. Now I have no way to work, or to the store, or to do anything I fuckin need to do." I told Marshon, resting the back of my head on his shoulder.

"On top of that, my mother has not come home and I really don't have any cash."

"Told you that little nigga was a waste of time, didn't I?" he gloated, and I just sighed again.

"But you know what; I'm not gone even say I told you so," he said kissing my neck.

I rolled my eyes because he had already said 'I told you so' twice.

"What time you have to be at work?" he asked.

"It doesn't even matter, because I don't have any way, and I need to go look for my mom and I just need a fuckin car." I told Marshon flopping back on his bed.

"Well you know I got a rental, and..."

"And I can't keep calling you when I need to come and go I have a lot of things to do," I told him cutting him off.

"That's not what the hell I was going to say. What I was going to say, before you cut me off, was that I got you. You can use the rental, for a couple days," Marshon said with a cocky smile.

He walked over to his night stand and grabbed the keys slapping them in my hand. He licked his lips and smiled.

"See I know how to take care of my girl unlike the wack ass nigga you been fuckin with," said Marshon.

I smiled and kissed Marshon's smooth cheek.

"Thanks Shon! You just saved my life." I told him, kissing his cheek again.

"Damn baby, that's all I get? Two kisses on the cheek?" he said, pulling me into his space.

"Baby you know I got a game tomorrow and I always play better when I'm relaxed," Marshon said running his hands through my hair.

"Oh, you need to *relax*, huh? Babe I would, but I just started my period,"

Marhson ran his finger over my mouth shutting me up.

"What's wrong with your lips?"

"Nothing," I said, feeling his lips on my neck.

"Please baby, scouts gone be at the game," he said, guiding me to my knees.

I knew what Marshon wanted; it wasn't like I had never done it before. I ran my hands up and down his legs talking myself into doing it. I sat the car key on the floor and placed both my hands in his pants. It was already hard and throbbing. My pussy was already starting to juice up looking at it. I held it with both hands and ran my tongue over the tip.

"Yeah baby," Marshon said, as I slipped the tip of my tongue in the opening tasting the pre cum.

I looked up at Marshon with his head tilted back and slid his whole pipe in to my mouth. Caressing his dick with both hands, I inched the entire thing into my mouth.

"Umm baby, daddy like," Shon said, as I removed my hands from his dick and pressed my hands on his back so he could push the whole thing down my throat.

Marshon liked to fuck me in my mouth so I closed my eyes and sucked hard while he pumped my mouth like it was my pussy. I started to moan as he tensed up and slowed his pace. I sped my pace up and began to take his breath away. Marshon gripped my hair with both hands and pushed himself so far down my throat that my stomach started to hurt! He then released all his juices. When he was done he let my hair go and fell backwards to the bed.

"Damn baby." Marshon said still trying to catch his breath.

I wiped my mouth with the back of my hand and stood to my feet. I dusted my knees off and picked the keys from the floor and bent to kiss Marshon's face.

"Thank you Shon," I said walking towards the door.

"You are leaving?" he asked, holding his hand out for me.

"Yeah. I work at like 7 A.M." I said, walking out of his bedroom, past his Mom and her blunt, and then out of the apartment.

I walked down the stairs to my apartment and rushed straight to the room. I placed the keys in my night stand, and rushed to the bathroom to take a hot shower. I made sure to brush my teeth twice. Then, I slipped on another pair of leggings and a body hugging T shirt. I grabbed the keys from my nightstand, and slipped into my sneakers as I ran out the door.

I was so excited as I ran down the stairs. A smile covered my entire face.

"Who is it?" a woman said snatching the door open.

That's when it hits me that it was after 1 A.M. and everyone was probably sleep.

"Hi, I'm Kalihia. I don't know if you remember me, but I'm Kre's friend. Sorry to bother ya'll so late, but I really needed to see Kre," I said looking at Kre's mother.

She looked at me, then stepped aside and reluctantly pointed to the back where Kre's room was. She wasn't like Marshon's mom who didn't mind people coming and going all hours into the night. I walked into Kre's bedroom, where he was lying in the bed with a pillow over his face in complete darkness. However, I could still see his baby blue boxers. That was all that he had on. I walked over to his bed and climbed on top of him kissing his lips.

"Fuck is you doing? Chill, yo." Kre said sitting up, as I kissed his cheek.

"Kre I'm not the other girl, I'm your girl and I got you! Always, no matter what I have to!" I told him, handing him the keys to Marshon's rental.

Kre looked from the keys to me and before he could ask any questions I lifted my shirt over my head and sat on Kre's lap facing him. I kissed his neck and ran my hands up his back. I knew we had shit to do, but the guilt I was feeling from sucking Marshon off could only be replaced with showing Kre that he was my man and I was all his.

Chapter 9

Kre

Kaihlia was straddled across me, with those thick thighs of hers pinning me down to my bed. She was rubbing her tits in my face, turning me on but I pushed her away gently.

"C'mon now, I said to chill with all that right now. What are you tryin' to do?" I whispered.

"What you think I'm tryin' to do?" she replied, with a smile.

"My Mom will come in here and beat both of our asses. We can't disrespect her crib like that. Plus, I got mad shit on my mind." I said, standing up from the bed.

"Ugh! It's like the more I try to get close to you, the more you push me away." Kaihlia said, frustrated as she could be.

"It's not like that. I just gotta find a way to figure out what the fuck is goin' on with Wes and Monique. That shit is really botherin' me. Something keeps telling me they had something to do with my brother getting' killed and I know that he would want me to ride for him." I said, as I continued to add up all the events surrounding Kre's death up in my head.

"Well let's go over there! You know where Wes lives and you seen the bitch Monique goin' into his house earlier, right? That's what I went and borrowed Marshon's keys for." explained Kaihlia.

Kaihlia just wanted to go over to Wes' crib, knock on the door and catch him and Monique laid up together. Did she not understand that Wes was a fuckin' G? That nigga had been in the streets since before I started kindergarten. He was thorough as hell, and Kaihlia expected a young nigga like me to just run up on him demanding answers. I didn't even have a gun and I was supposed to threaten this nigga Wes who was almost 10 years older than me and twice my size? I was convinced Kaihlia just didn't know how things worked in the street.

"What? You scared or somethin'?" she asked, sensing the fear in my eyes.

"Nah, I ain't scared of shit!" I barked back, kind of offended that she would come at me like that.

Kaihlia just looked down at the keys again.

"Fuck is you waitin' for then? Let's ride." she said, almost like she was daring me.

The truth is, I was nervous about making a move like that, but I couldn't look like a bitch in front of Kaihlia. I slipped on an all black Champion hoodie and some jeans and motioned for Kaihlia to come on.

"Where the hell ya'll goin?" my Mom asked as we headed for the door.

She was already on edge after losing Keon a few days ago, so watching me walk out of the house in the middle of the night had her even more stressed.

"I'll be back. I just gotta handle somethin' real fast," I nonchalantly said.

"Ugh! As if I ain't under enough stress thinking about this funeral!" screamed my Mom, who had apparently reached her breaking point.

"Mom, just relax!" I said, with some bass in my voice.

"Relax? I done already lost one son and now you lookin' like you about to go get into some crazy shit!" she hollered back.

I just stood still and let my Mom vent as Kaihlia looked on. She had no idea my Mom could get so turned up since she was usually always quiet.

"What's goin' on?" asked Kenya, as she groggily stumbled into the living room.

"You see? All this mess you got goin' on done woke ya sister up!" continued my Mom.

I heard what my Mom was saying, but I had to do what I had to do. It was time to be a man, and ride for my brother Keon. He deserved that. Keon had been there for me after the rooftop incident, so I owed it to him to get to the bottom of this situation. I believed Wes and Monique had set him up in some way or the other, and I was out to prove it.

"I'll be back, Mom. I promise you that." I said, as I took Kaihlia's arm and headed towards the front door.

*****

I couldn't even hate; Marshon's rented SUV was pretty dope. It was a 2014 Audi Q5 and the interior was laced with Nappa leather and a wood grain dash. The car even had XM radio, but I wasn't in the mood to listen to much music. As Kaihlia drove the big boy truck, all I could think about was what I was going to say to Wes and Monique. They both should have been ashamed of themselves since they said they supposedly had love for Keon.

After what seemed like only a few minutes, Kaihlia pulled onto Wes' block.

"Turn the lights off and just drive by real slow," I said, my voice unintentionally cracking with fear.

"Man, fuck that! We goin' in there and confront them. Man up, yo." said Kaihlia, hype as hell.

"Man up?" Who did this broad think she was talking to? Kaihlia had a lot of nerve. She was talking to me like I was some young ass, wet behind the ears nigga, but I had been running the streets with my brother and Monique for the past few months. I knew what I was doing, but she insisted on doing things her way.

Instead of pulling up slow, Kaihlia pulled up in front of Wes' house at full speed. She put the car in park and before I knew it she had hopped out and was heading towards the front door. Meanwhile, I was taking a second to survey the scene and add everything up. Wes' Tahoe was nowhere to be seen, but my brother's BMW was parked right in front of the house. Inside, the living room light was on, so I figured Monique was in there all alone.

'Good' I thought to myself, realizing that I wouldn't have to deal with Wes for time being.

Kaihlia got to the front door first and immediately started banging on it.

"Yo, open up bitch! I see you in there. Wake the fuck up!" hollered Kaihlia, as she looked through the window and saw Monique lying on the couch.

As loud as Kaihlia was, Monique didn't move.

"Give me your hoodie," said Kaihlia.

"Huh?" I asked, confused.

"Just give it to me," said Kaihlia, with her hand out.

I took off the hoodie and handed it to Kaihlia. She wrapped it around her hand and then cocked back and struck the glass part of Wes' front door a few times. After a few blows, the glass broke she reached her hand inside. She had used my hoodie to soften the blow and prevent her hand from getting cut up on the glass.

I just looked at Kaihlia in awe. This chic was crazy!

"Have you done this before?" I asked, as Kaihlia unlocked the door from the inside.

"Maybe." she smiled.

Just like that, we were inside the house, staring at Monique who was still laid on the couch. She had always been a heavy sleeper when we lived together in the old apartment. Me and Keon used to stay up half the night playing Playstation and blasting music and she could sleep through all of that, so I wasn't totally shocked that we hadn't awakened her.

On the table next to the couch Monique was lying on was an empty bottle of wine, her Louie Vuitton purse, and a short handwritten note. While Kaihlia crept over toward Monique, I quickly read the note.

Mo,

I had to handle some business with the new connect. I'll be back in the morning, but I left you a bottle of Moscato in the fridge.

Love,

Wes

If there was any more doubt that Monique and Wes were fucking, the note cleared that all up. They definitely had a relationship. I could only wonder how long it had been going on. As Kaihlia examined Monique, I was amazed that she still hadn't woken up.

"Yo, is she still asleep?" I asked Kaihlia, as she got up close to Monique.

"Nah, this bitch ain't sleep. She's dead!" said Kaihlia, as she checked Monique's pulse.

I panicked like hell. Monique's eyes were rolled back into the back of her head. She was most certainly dead, and Kaihlia and I were in the house with the body.

"We gotta get the fuck up out of here!" I said.

Kaihlia agreed, but made some quick suggestions.

"Get your brother's keys." she said.

I quickly scanned the room looking for the BMW key. After all, the car didn't belong to Monique, and in her condition she would never be needing it again. After a few seconds, I found the key fob on the kitchen table and scooped it up.

"Let's go," I said, as I led the way out of the house.

"Hold up," said Kaihlia, as she doubled back.

"Fuck is you doin'?" I asked, ready to be out.

"Shit, I want that Louie bag!"

Typical woman shit, I thought to myself. In the midst of some crazy shit and all she was thinking about was fashion. Kaihlia scooped up the bag and ran across the room.

"Any money in there?" I asked, as Kaihlia headed in my direction.

Kaihlia paused for a second to open the purse.

"Oh shit!" she hollered.

"What?" I asked.

Kaihlia showed me the inside of the purse; racks on racks on racks! All I saw were hundred dollar bills wrapped in rubber band stacks. I didn't know how much was in the bag just by looking, but I knew that my Mom wouldn't have to stress over paying for Keon's funeral anymore.

"Meet me back at your apartment," I said, as I bolted for the door.

"Kre, wait!" said Kaihlia.